ISSUES THAT CONCERN YOU

Divorce and Children

Maria L. Howell, *Book Editor*

GREENHAVEN PRESS
A part of Gale, Cengage Learning

GALE
CENGAGE Learning

Detroit • New York • San Francisco • New Haven, Conn • Waterville, Maine • London

GALE
CENGAGE Learning™

Christine Nasso, *Publisher*
Elizabeth Des Chenes, *Managing Editor*

© 2009 Greenhaven Press, a part of Gale, Cengage Learning

Gale and Greenhaven Press are registered trademarks used herein under license.

For more information, contact:
Greenhaven Press
27500 Drake Rd.
Farmington Hills, MI 48331-3535
Or you can visit our Internet site at gale.cengage.com

Articles in Greenhaven Press anthologies are often edited for length to meet page requirements. In addition, original titles of these works are changed to clearly present the main thesis and to explicitly indicate the author's opinion. Every effort is made to ensure that Greenhaven Press accurately reflects the original intent of the authors. Every effort has been made to trace the owners of copyrighted material.

Cover image copyright Tatiana, Gladskikh, 2009. Used under license from Shutterstock.

LIBRARY OF CONGRESS CATALOGING-IN-PUBLICATION DATA

Divorce and children / Maria L. Howell, book editor.
   p. cm. -- (Issues that concern you)
 Includes bibliographical references and index.
 ISBN 978-0-7377-4185-8 (hardcover)
 1. Divorce. 2. Children of divorced parents. I. Howell, Maria L.
 HQ814.D62 2009
 306.89--dc22

                                           2008050587

Printed in the United States of America
1 2 3 4 5 6 7 13 12 11 10 09

CONTENTS

I still remember like it was yesterday; my brother and I were playing in our "playroom," and we got a call from our parents to come out into the living room. They were each sitting at one end of our maroon couch, and told us to sit down between them. Even at my young age, I knew that something was not right. Little did I know that soon I was going to realize that I was not going to grow up in the typical American family that most of my friends and family were accustomed to. My parents told us that they had decided to get a divorce. My dad was going to move out, and my brother and I were going to live at home with Mom. . . . This is one of the two times I have ever seen my father cry, not because he was sad about the divorce necessarily, but because he was not going to be living with his children anymore.[1]

For children, the scars of their parents' divorce may heal, but like the anonymous writer in the narrative above, the feelings of utter devastation, of profound loss and sadness at the breakup of their families, are always with them and always will be. "The divorce up to this point in my life is the hardest thing I have ever had to go through," the young man continues. "I think that only the death of my parents or siblings could be more difficult. The long term effects of the divorce are still not completely gone and probably never will be."[2]

According to recent studies, over 1 million children in the United States will experience the divorce of their parents this year. For parents, divorce is the ending of one chapter in their lives and the beginning of another. For children, however, divorce is different. Studies show that for at least the first two years, divorce can shatter a child's universe, setting him or her adrift on an ocean of uncertainty and distress. Will I see my father again? Will my mother be able to take care of me? Do I get to see my friends again? How much damage divorce does, however, has been the subject of much research and debate. Some research shows that the effects of divorce have consequences that go well beyond adolescence and into adulthood. Other studies show that while children are in danger of developing emotional problems, parental divorce will not lead to a child's lifelong problems.

Clinical psychologist Judith Wallerstein, widely considered the world's foremost authority on the effects of divorce, argues in her book *The Unexpected Legacy of Divorce* that children experience the greatest impact of their parents' divorce during adulthood. She states that through no fault of their own, children of divorced families have little or no knowledge of how to sustain a romantic relationship or how to resolve conflicts that arise in those relationships. To make matters worse, she adds, many young adults enter relationships with high expectations, only to end up being bitterly disillusioned. A young girl called Karen seems to confirm Wallerstein's theories as she explains why she moved in with her boyfriend, Nick. "I'm not sure. I knew I didn't love him. But I was scared of marriage. I was scared of divorce, and I'm terrified of being alone. Look, you can hope for love but you can't expect it. When Nick asked me to live with him, I was afraid that I'd get older and that I wouldn't have another chance. I kept thinking that I'd end up lonely like my dad. And Mom." Wallerstein contends that having watched their parents dissolve their marriages, children from divorced families simply are not mindful of the enormous effort entailed in preserving a marriage. Unlike children from intact marriages, who garner fortitude and courage from their parents, Wallerstein argues that children from divorced families are anxious and fearful over their relationships. "There's another reason I moved in with him," Karen continues quite bashfully. "I figured that this is one man who will never leave me. Because he has no ambitions, he will always have fewer choices than me. So if I stay with him and even marry him someday, I won't ever have to worry about his walking out."[3]

Penn State sociology professor Paul Amato, who has researched divorce and children for the last twenty years, has a

Adult children of divorced families have little or no knowledge of how to sustain a romantic relationship or how to resolve conflicts within that relationship.

different take on the long-term effects of divorce on children. While he essentially concurs with Wallerstein's "sleeper effect" theory—that conflicts arise as children reach adulthood—he finds her conclusions too negative and pessimistic. He argues that most scientific research shows that although divorce may affect children negatively, they are not all doomed to lead a terrible life.

Author Elizabeth Marquardt contends that parental divorce may indeed have long-term consequences for children, particularly as it relates to how they view and understand themselves. In her book *Between Two Worlds: The Inner Lives of Children of Divorce*, Marquardt argues that children of divorced families are trapped between parents' opposing values, beliefs, and lifestyles. As a result, she asserts, they feel confused and alone, since these conflicting values strike at the very heart of their identity. Fundamental questions such as "Who am I?" and "What are my values?" become a moral dilemma for children of divorce.

With divorce on the rise in the United States, the debate on its long-term effects on children will continue. In *Issues That Concern You: Divorce and Children*, the authors present a variety of perspectives on this subject.

In addition, the volume includes a bibliography, a list of organizations to contact for further information, and other useful appendixes. The appendix titled "What You Should Know About Divorce and Children" offers vital facts about divorce and how it affects young people. The appendix "What You Should Do About Divorce" discusses various solutions to the problem of divorce. These many useful features make *Issues That Concern You: Divorce and Children* a valuable resource. Given the growing social and financial costs of divorce to society, having a greater understanding of this issue is critical.

1. Quoted in John H. Harvey and Mark Fine, *Children of Divorce: Stories of Loss and Growth*. Mahwah, NJ: Erlbaum, 2004, p. 77.
2. Quoted in Harvey and Fine, p. 78.
3. Judith S. Wallerstein, Julia Lewis, and Sandra Blakeslee, *The Unexpected Legacy of Divorce*. New York: Hyperion, 2000, p. 294.

ONE

Divorce Does Not Impact All Children the Same Way

Alison Clarke-Stewart and Cornelia Brentano

In their book *Divorce: Causes and Consequences*, from which the following essay is excerpted, Alison Clarke-Stewart and Cornelia Brentano analyze the behaviors of children in order to determine how children from divorced families function when compared with children whose parents are married. The authors conclude that children of parental divorce are "two or three times more likely to have problems." These problems include behavior issues, self-esteem concerns, lack of motivation to succeed academically, and difficulties adjusting socially and psychologically. Clarke-Stewart and Brentano claim that although these differences are somewhat small and are not experienced equally by all children, or in the same manner, the differences remain constant throughout various studies and are statistically important. Despite this fact, they argue that only a small number of these children sustain long-term effects that continue into adulthood. Clarke-Stewart is professor of psychology and social behavior at the University of California, Irvine. Brentano is an assistant professor of psychology at Chapman University in Orange, California.

Nearly half of the children born to married parents in this country go through a divorce experience before they are eighteen—about one million children each year. For these children, even more than for their parents, divorce can be an extraordinarily difficult experience. For adults, a divorce may offer advantages—pursuit of a new career, a new hobby, a new spouse, or a new lover. For them, the divorce, although painful, can be a net gain. But children see no benefit in divorce. The end of their parents' marriage is a complete loss, turning their lives upside down. Reactions vary with age, but across the board, children experience feelings of confusion and betrayal as they watch their family fall apart and feel neglected while their parents struggle with their own problems. They just wish their parents would get back together and shape up. But, beyond these initial

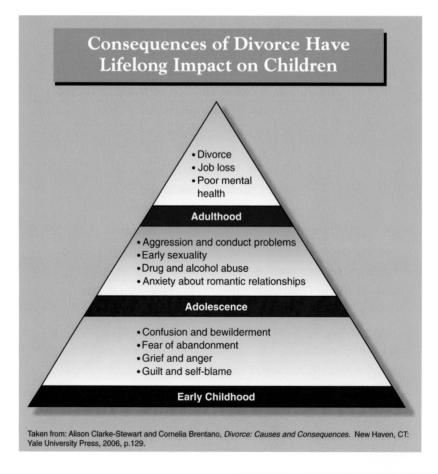

Consequences of Divorce Have Lifelong Impact on Children

- Divorce
- Job loss
- Poor mental health

Adulthood

- Aggression and conduct problems
- Early sexuality
- Drug and alcohol abuse
- Anxiety about romantic relationships

Adolescence

- Confusion and bewilderment
- Fear of abandonment
- Grief and anger
- Guilt and self-blame

Early Childhood

Taken from: Alison Clarke-Stewart and Cornelia Brentano, *Divorce: Causes and Consequences*. New Haven, CT: Yale University Press, 2006, p.129.

reactions, how much does divorce affect children in the long run? Do they suffer permanent psychological and physical problems? Do they have trouble in school? Are they "victims" of the breakup in the same way some adults are? . . .

Differences Between Children in Divorced and Nondivorced Families

The main goal of research on children of divorce has been to compare the functioning of these children with that of children in intact, two-parent families. These comparisons provide ample evidence that children from divorced families have more behavioral, emotional, health, and academic problems. As we will see, the differences are not large and they are not necessarily permanent; nor are all children affected equally. But the differences are consistent across studies and statistically significant. Compared with children in intact families, children from divorced families are more likely to have conduct problems and show signs of psychological maladjustment; they have lower academic achievement, more social difficulties, and poorer self-esteem. Because so much research has been conducted in this area, researchers have been able to combine findings from multiple studies in meta-analyses, in which the results of separate studies are expressed in terms of a common "effect size" representing the difference between children in divorced and intact families. One of these meta-analyses, published by Paul Amato in 1991, combined the results of ninety-two studies in which researchers had compared the well-being of children living in divorced, single-parent families with that of children living in continuously intact families. In 70 percent of these studies, children with divorced parents had lower levels of well-being than children in intact families. The largest differences were in the areas of aggressive conduct and poor social adjustment, although significant differences also indicated that children from divorced families did more poorly in school achievement and psychological adjustment.

These meta-analyses were updated by Amato in 2001 with results from sixty-seven new studies. The new studies were more sophisticated than those in earlier decades; they included larger, more representative samples and national, longitudinal data sets such as the National Longitudinal Survey of Youth, the National Study of Families and Households, the High School and Beyond Study, and the British National Longitudinal Study. The new studies also included smaller but more intensively studied longitudinal samples, and they included prospective studies—that is, studies that started before people even got divorced, which made it possible to control statistically for such factors as parents' predivorce income and children's predivorce behavior for problems. Despite these improvements in the available research, results from the 2001 meta-analyses were strikingly similar to those from 1991. As in the earlier meta-analyses, on average, children with divorced parents did significantly worse than children with continuously married parents in terms of academic achievement, self-esteem, popularity and peer relations, misbehavior, depression, and anxiety.

These meta-analyses focused on children's psychological well-being because this is what has been studied most frequently by psychologists. However, differences have also been found in children's physical health. Their parents rate them as being less healthy, and the children themselves report more physical symptoms. A link with diabetes has been found: 40 percent of children with diabetes had gone through a divorce before the onset of the disease, compared with only 17 percent of a randomly selected comparison group from the same community.

Researchers have also discovered that there are more subtle costs for children when they have to cope with their parents' divorce, costs that do not necessarily show up on standard tests of achievement, behavior, or health. These emotional costs include embarrassment, fear of abandonment, grief over loss, irrational hope of reconciliation, worry about their parents' well-being, anxiety about divided loyalties, and uncertainty about romantic relationships. In the early years after their parents' divorce, all children feel sad and almost all feel angry, and these feelings do not disappear easily. In one study of college students, researchers found that those who had experienced their parents' divorce reported distressing feelings, beliefs, and experiences. These were resilient young people and the divorce had occurred years earlier, but still they harbored painful feelings. They were functioning well enough to be attending college, and their scores on standardized measures of depression and anxiety were not elevated, but they struggled with inner fears, worries, and regrets. Three-quarters of them said that they felt they would have been a different person if their parents had not gotten divorced. Half said they worried about events like graduation or weddings when both of their parents would be present. Half said they missed not having their father

"Thanks to separations, divorces and remarriages, I've got 20 grandparents."

"Thanks to separations, divorces and remarriages, I've got 20 grandparents." Cartoon by Mike Baldwin. www.CartoonStock.Com.

around, they had a harder childhood than most people, or they wished they had grown up in a never-divorced family. One quarter wondered whether their father really loved them, and one-fifth believed they were doomed to repeat their parents' problems. These students' responses were significantly different from those of students who grew up in always-married families.

It is clear from this plethora of studies that divorce has some negative emotional, social, physical, and cognitive effects on some children. In this [viewpoint] we discuss these negative effects for children at different ages. In considering these negative consequences of divorce, however, it is important to keep in mind that many—in fact most—divorce "victims" are functioning well despite their earlier experiences and emotions. . . .

The Impact on Adolescents

Early adolescence is a vulnerable time at best—a time of shaky self-esteem and autonomy issues. When their parents divorce, young adolescents often overreact with unrealistic anguish and anxiety. In their adolescent egocentrism they can see only their own needs and they feel that the world's eyes are on them. So they lash out at their parents, "How could you do this to *me?*" They are preoccupied with shame and embarrassment and more self-conscious than adolescents from intact families. Rarely do they understand their parents' perspective. They express harsh moral judgments against their parents as they become aware of the adults' weaknesses and failures.

To make matters worse, their parents often give these young adolescents added household and child-care responsibilities and urge them to take on odd jobs to make some extra money. Young adolescents often see themselves as having to mature faster because of divorce. As a result, the entire divorce experience can lead young adolescents to have a sense of "false maturity." They identify with the custodial parent and take on the role of the departed parent: an adolescent son becomes the man around the house; an adolescent girl becomes the parent's confidant. Often, they have to listen as their parents unload their feelings of misery and frustration. This early push for maturity comes with a high price tag. Being cast into a role for which they are not ready may lead young adolescents to be depressed. It is all too much for them. They cannot hide behind the confusion of the preschool child or erupt into the angry outbursts of the school-age child. They understand what is going on, but they are helpless to stop it. They are angry about their lack of control and may engage in risky behaviors, such as sex, drugs, and alcohol. Looking for love and attention to cover their pain and loss, seeing their parents dating, and lacking strict parental supervision, these young adolescents can be thrust into premature sexual activity—just as they are entering puberty. The consequences of these risky behaviors may be substantial—early pregnancy, problems in school, trouble with the law. Remember, though, that we are talking about increases in the *likelihood* of these problems for children of divorce; not all young adolescents experience these difficulties.

Older Adolescents Get in Trouble

Older adolescents (fifteen- to eighteen-year-olds) may not experience their parents' divorce to be as earth shattering as it is for younger ones because their egos are more mature. They are more involved in their own activities, more independent of their parents. Nevertheless, even these older adolescents often have strong reactions when their parents divorce. They may feel abandoned, anxious, and depressed. Their use of drugs and alcohol may increase. They may have problems sleeping and eating and focusing on their work or studies. They may have problems with interpersonal relationships. Older adolescents are preoccupied with issues of their own identity: this is the time when they try to figure out who they are. They need to develop a self-image as a unique person so that they can enter adulthood with self-confidence and a clear idea of their personal goals and values. When parents divorce, especially if the divorce is unexpected, adolescents' developing identity can be thrown into chaos and their self-confidence may be undermined.

Without a clear path to a mature identity, adolescents can find a variety of ways to get in trouble. One place they may get into trouble is in school. Studies show that adolescents from divorced families get lower grades, do more poorly on achievement tests, and have lower educational aspirations than adolescents in intact families. In one longitudinal study in Iowa, children from divorced families were at least twice as likely as those from intact families to have academic difficulties—they got more Ds and Fs, had trouble keeping up with their classes, and had less sense of mastery in their academic subjects. Perhaps even more important, adolescents from divorced families are twice as likely to drop out of school as those from intact families. In a study that has been ongoing for ten years and covers ten large survey data sets, the high school dropout risk for adolescents whose parents divorced when they were between twelve and twenty years of age was 27 percent, compared with 13 percent for children in intact families. As this finding shows, the risk of dropping out of school is significantly greater for adolescents whose parents divorce, but still the majority—73 percent—are not dropouts.

Adolescents from divorced families may also get into trouble with other people. They are not as socially competent as adolescents from intact families, according to their teachers and their mothers. Worse, they often have behavior problems. For one thing, they are more aggressive and antisocial. Their mothers and teachers notice this and so do trained observers; the adolescents themselves also admit it. They say that they have committed more delinquent acts—shoplifting, damaging school property, running away from home, getting drunk in a public place, fighting, stealing, being stopped or picked up by the police, hurting someone enough to need bandaging, telling lies about something important. In the Iowa study, 17 percent of the boys and 8 percent of the girls from divorced families versus only 4 percent and 3 percent of the boys and girls from intact families admitted to having committed at least six delinquent acts in the previous year. They were also more likely than adolescents from intact families to have sex—more than twice as likely if they were girls and four times as likely if they were boys. They were more likely to smoke and to use other drugs. Not only do adolescents from divorced families have these "externalizing" problems, they may also have "internalizing" problems. They are more anxious, withdrawn, and depressed than adolescents in intact families. They have less self-esteem. They more often have a sense of despair, and they are twice as likely to feel hopeless (30 percent versus 14 percent) or to think of ending their lives (16 percent versus 8 percent) as adolescents whose parents are happily married. It is a testament to the resilience of children that so many fare so well under adverse circumstances. The majority do not commit crimes, abuse substances, or think about suicide. . . .

Divorce has a stronger effect on problem behavior and psychological distress than race, birth order, moving, having a new sibling, experiencing the illness or death of a significant family member, being ill, or having parents with little education. It has a stronger effect on teen pregnancy than exposure to family violence in early childhood, low family income, and a low level of education. The association is larger than the link between smoking and cancer. This is not a problem we should blow out of proportion, but it is not a problem we should ignore. Instead, we should try to understand how we can reduce its negative impacts and predict which children will be adversely affected and in what ways. We will then be better able to help these children adjust to this life transition. . . .

It is important to keep these divorce effects in perspective. Although the differences between children from divorced and intact families are consistent and statistically significant, they are not large. Children of divorce are two or three times more likely to have problems than children from intact families, but this still means that only one-fifth to one-third of them have persistent problems. In adulthood, the number may be as low as one-tenth. The consequences of divorce, in short, do not affect all children in the same way or to the same degree, but for a significant minority there may be long-lasting effects that persist through adulthood.

TWO

Divorce Has a Lifelong Impact on Children

Judith S. Wallerstein, Julia Lewis, and Sandra Blakeslee

Judith S. Wallerstein is a clinical psychologist and the founder and executive director of the Center for the Family in Transition. She is emerita senior lecturer at the School of Social Welfare at the University of California at Berkeley. She has coauthored many books, which include the following: *Surviving the Breakup: How Children and Parents Cope With Divorce*; *Second Chances: Men, Women and Children a Decade After Divorce*; and *The Good Marriage: How and Why Love Lasts*. Julia Lewis is a colleague of Wallerstein and is also on the clinical psychology staff at San Francisco State University. Sandra Blakeslee is an award-winning science writer for *The New York Times* and the coauthor of *Second Chances*. In their book, *The Unexpected Legacy of Divorce*, the authors assert that although the impact of divorce on children intensifies at each stage of their development, it is in adulthood, as children search out romantic relationships, that parental divorce has its greatest effect. Wallerstein asserts that having witnessed the dissolution of their parents' marriage, children from divorced families enter adulthood with little or no skill in how to sustain a romantic relationship or even how to handle conflicts within that relationship. Unlike children from intact families, Wallerstein argues, children from divorced families simply are not aware of the sacrifices needed to sustain a good relationship. She asserts that while children from intact families found strength and courage from their parents' marriage because they stayed together despite conflicts and setbacks, children of parental divorce are filled with anxiety about their relationships, afraid of being abandoned, betrayed, and rejected.

From the viewpoint of the children, and counter to what happens to their parents, divorce is a cumulative experience. Its impact increases over time and rises to a crescendo in adulthood. At each developmental stage divorce is experienced anew in different ways. In adulthood it affects personality, the ability to

Adult children from divorced families are at a disadvantage due to anxiety about relationships and fear of abandonment, betrayal, and rejection.

trust, expectations about relationships, and ability to cope with change. . . .

As the children told us, adolescence begins early in divorced homes and, compared with that of youngsters raised in intact families, is more likely to include more early sexual experiences for girls and higher alcohol and drug use for girls and boys. Adolescence is more prolonged in divorced families and extends well into the years of early adulthood. Throughout these years children of divorce worry about following in their parents' footsteps and struggle with a sinking sense that they, too, will fail in their relationships.

But it's in adulthood that children of divorce suffer the most. The impact of divorce hits them most cruelly as they go in search of love, sexual intimacy, and commitment. Their lack of inner images of a man and a woman in a stable relationship and their memories of their parents' failure to sustain the marriage badly hobbles their search, leading them to heartbreak and even despair. They cried, "No one taught me." They complain bitterly that they feel unprepared for adult relationships and that they have never seen a "man and woman on the same beam," that they have no good models on which to build their hopes. And indeed they have a very hard time formulating even simple ideas about the kind of person they're looking for. Many end up with unsuitable or very troubled partners in relationships that were doomed from the start.

Intact Homes Versus Divorced Homes

The contrast between them and children from good intact homes, as both go in search of love and commitment, is striking. (. . . Children raised in extremely unhappy or violent intact homes face misery in childhood and tragic challenges in adulthood. But because their parents generally aren't interested in getting a divorce, divorce does not become part of their legacy.) Adults in their twenties from reasonably good or even moderately unhappy intact families had a fine understanding of the demands and sacrifices required in a close relationship. They had memories of how their parents struggled and overcame differences, how they cooperated in a crisis. They developed a general idea about the kind of person they wanted to marry. Most important, they did not expect to fail. The two groups differed after marriage as well. Those from intact families found the example of their parents' enduring marriage very reassuring when they inevitably ran into marital problems. But in coping with the normal stresses in a marriage, adults from divorced families were at a grave disadvantage. Anxiety about relationships was at the bedrock of their personalities and endured even in very happy marriages. Their fears of disaster and sudden loss rose when they felt content. And their fear of abandonment, betrayal, and rejection mounted when they found themselves having to disagree with someone they loved. After all, marriage is a slippery slope and their parents fell off it. All had trouble dealing with differences or even moderate contact in their close relationships. Typically their first response was panic, often followed by flight. They had a lot to undo and a lot to learn in a very short time.

Those who had two parents who rebuilt happy lives after divorce and included children in their orbits had a much easier time as adults. Those who had committed single parents also benefited from that parent's attention and responsiveness. But the more frequent response in adulthood was continuing anger at parents, more often at fathers, whom the children regarded as having been selfish and faithless.

Others felt deep compassion and pity toward mothers or fathers who failed to rebuild their lives after divorce. The ties between daughters and their mothers were especially close but at a cost. Some young women found it very difficult to separate from their moms and to lead their own lives. With some notable exceptions, fathers in divorced families were less likely to enjoy close bonds with their adult children, especially their sons. This stood in marked contrast to fathers and sons from intact families, who tended to grow closer as the years went by.

Fortunately for many children of divorce, their fears of loss and betrayal can be conquered by the time they reach their late twenties and thirties. But what a struggle that takes, what courage and persistence. Those who succeed overcome their difficulties the hard way—by learning from their own failed relationships and gradually rejecting the models they were raised with to create what they

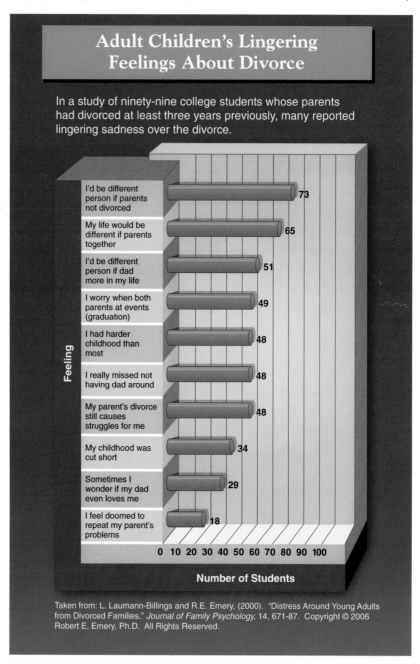

Adult Children's Lingering Feelings About Divorce

In a study of ninety-nine college students whose parents had divorced at least three years previously, many reported lingering sadness over the divorce.

I'd be different person if parents not divorced — 73
My life would be different if parents together — 65
I'd be different person if dad more in my life — 51
I worry when both parents at events (graduation) — 49
I had harder childhood than most — 48
I really missed not having dad around — 48
My parent's divorce still causes struggles for me — 48
My childhood was cut short — 34
Sometimes I wonder if my dad even loves me — 29
I feel doomed to repeat my parent's problems — 18

Feeling

0 10 20 30 40 50 60 70 80 90 100

Number of Students

Taken from: L. Laumann-Billings and R.E. Emery, (2000). "Distress Around Young Adults from Divorced Families," *Journal of Family Psychology*, 14, 671-87. Copyright © 2006 Robert E. Emery, Ph.D. All Rights Reserved.

want from a love relationship. Those lucky enough to have found a loving partner are able to interrupt their self-destructive course with a lasting love affair or marriage.

Economics of Divorce

In other realms of adult life—financial and security, for instance—some children were able to overcome difficulties through unexpected help from fathers who had vanished long before. Still others benefit from the constancy of parents or grandparents. Many men and women raised in divorced families establish successful careers. Their workplace performance is largely unaffected by the divorce. But no matter what their success in the world, they retain some serious residues—fear of loss, fear of change, and fear that disaster will strike, especially when things are going well. They're still terrified by the mundane differences and inevitable conflicts found in every close relationship.

I'm heartened by the hard-won success of these adults. But at the same time, I can't forget those who've failed to straighten out their lives. I'm especially troubled by how many divorced or remained in wretched marriages. Of those who have children and who are now divorced, many, to my dismay, are not protecting their children in ways we might expect. They go on to repeat the same mistakes their own parents made, perpetuating problems that have plagued them all their lives. I'm also concerned about many who, by their mid- and late thirties, are neither married nor cohabiting and who are leading lonely lives. They're afraid of getting involved in a relationship that they think is doomed to fail. After a divorce or breakup, they're afraid to try again. And I'm struck by continuing anger at parents and flat-out statements by many of these young adults that they have no intention of helping their moms and especially their dads or stepparents in old age. This may change. But if it doesn't, we'll be facing another unanticipated consequence of our divorce culture. Who will take care of an older generation estranged from its children?

THREE

Divorce May Not Cause Children's Behavior Problems

Sharon Jayson

In the following article, "Study: Divorce May Not Cause Kids' Bad Behavior," author Sharon Jayson examines the findings of a recent study, *The Kids Are OK: Divorce and Children's Behavior Problems*, in which Jui-Chung Allen Li of the RAND Corporation asserts that no causal link between parental divorce and a child's behavior exists. Social scientist Robert Emery, Jayson adds, concurs that previous research has been "simplistic" in its findings that divorce is the source of children's problems. However, Emery concludes that Li's findings "are too strong." Divorce is always a risk to children's development, Emery states. These sentiments are echoed by other social scientists and researchers that Jayson cites. Jayson is a writer for *USA Today*.

Divorce often gets blamed for a host of troubles faced by children whose parents split, and much past research has focused on the damage to children's well-being.

But new research suggests that at least in one segment of overall well-being—bad behavior—divorce doesn't appear to be the reason for some behavior problems.

"It really depends on the individual marriages and the family," says [Jui-Chung] Allen Li, associate director of the Population Research Center at the RAND Corporation in Santa Monica, Calif. "My conclusion is that divorce is neither bad nor good."

His findings, to be presented Saturday in Chicago at a meeting of the non-profit Council on Contemporary Families, contrast with a body of research about divorce's effect on children that some researchers say has overestimated the difficulty that parents' divorce causes for children.

Other Experts Respond

A review of marriage research released in a 2005 journal published by the Brookings Institution and Princeton University suggested that children from two-parent families are better off emotionally, socially and economically. Other research, released

Research done by the Brookings Institution and Princeton University suggests that children from two-parent families are better off emotionally, socially, and economically than children of one-parent families.

the same year in a book by Elizabeth Marquardt, a vice president at the conservative Institute for American Values in New York, found that an unhappy marriage without a lot of conflict is better for children than divorce.

Others, including Robert Emery of the University of Virginia at Charlottesville, agree that much past research has been overly simplistic in assuming divorce causes the behavior problems. But he adds that he believes Li's conclusions "are too strong."

"Divorce still does have consequences for kids," he says.

Li's study of 6,332 children is significant for its large sample, as well as a new statistical model used in the analysis. Also, unlike many previous studies on the effect of divorce on children, Li doesn't compare the children of married parents with the

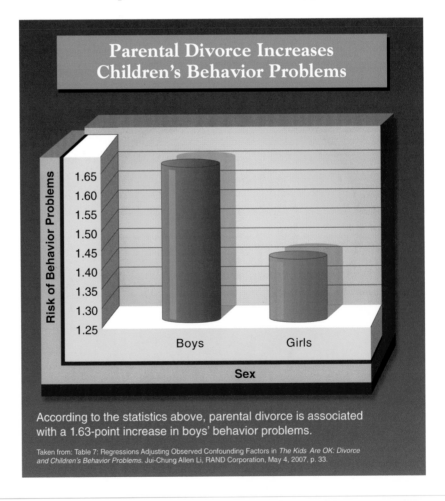

Parental Divorce Increases Children's Behavior Problems

According to the statistics above, parental divorce is associated with a 1.63-point increase in boys' behavior problems.

Taken from: Table 7: Regressions Adjusting Observed Confounding Factors in *The Kids Are OK: Divorce and Children's Behavior Problems.* Jui-Chung Allen Li, RAND Corporation, May 4, 2007, p. 33.

children of divorced parents. Rather, he took a longitudinal approach and examined children's behavior before and after their parents split.

His 28-item checklist measured behavior problems, such as crying, cheating or arguing frequently, from ages 4 to 15. He found a slight post-divorce increase in bad behavior that he says is so small it is not statistically significant. The trajectory of misbehavior that started before the divorce might well have continued, even if the parents had not divorced, he says.

By contrast, Marquardt compared the children of divorced families with those of married parents. She defends that approach as valid. "What he's doing is controlling for so many things he's making the effects of divorce disappear," she says. "People like me have some real qualms about that."

In the early 1990s, research by social demographer Andrew Cherlin of Johns Hopkins University in Baltimore looked at children before and after parents divorced and compared them with children with married parents. He found that some of the problems children showed after the divorce were apparent before the split.

"Some of the problems we attribute to divorce are present before a child's parents divorce. The implication is they might have happened anyway," he says. "Not all of the problems children of divorce show are due to divorce."

But he says that's not the whole story.

"My line on this is that most children are not seriously affected by divorce in the long-term, but divorce raises the risk that a child will have problems," Cherlin says.

FOUR

Divorce Can Have a Positive Effect on Children

Max Sindell

Max Sindell is a recent graduate of Johns Hopkins University. In his work *The Bright Side: Surviving Your Parents' Divorce*, excerpted below, Sindell argues that although parental divorce may destabilize children in many ways, this experience may in fact be the catalyst to an even richer and fuller life. To begin with, Sindell states that the divorce of his parents provided him with opportunities to travel and explore new places, such as Colorado, where his father moved and where he learned to ski. In addition, he would never have had the experience of living in a downtown apartment in a large city or attending a boarding school if his parents had remained married. Most of all, traveling provided opportunities to bond with his "single parents" and get to know them in ways he would not have done prior to the divorce. Sindell also asserts that since divorced parents have to work, children from divorced families become responsible at an early age, a milestone that children from intact families may not achieve until much later in life.

When your parents split, it's possible that one of them will move to a new city or state. And while that can be difficult to deal with at first, it brings with it thousands of new experiences. If my parents hadn't divorced, I would have never known about Aspen, Colorado. I would never have learned to ski. I would never have learned to travel by myself at eight years old. I would never have had the opportunity to explore Colorado with my father. I'd have never lived in an apartment in the middle of a major city. I probably would have never ended up going to boarding school. Maybe I'd have never even moved up to San Francisco. All these experiences have greatly affected my life, and I'm thankful for them every day. I wouldn't trade them for anything.

Also, realize that it's a unique opportunity to travel and explore with a single parent, and it can greatly change and strengthen your relationship. Most kids are outside of the decision-making circle or are just along for the ride while their parents travel together. Parents will always be parents, but it's those kinds of situations that can allow you and your parents to be friends as well as family.

You Will Have More Independence

Because your parents will have to spend more time worrying about themselves, they'll have less time to spend worrying about and taking care of you. I don't mean this to sound like bad news. What I mean is, since they can't take care of you all the time, you'll get to start taking care of yourself.

You will be listened to more often. Your parents want to make sure that everything is all right with you, that you are okay. This can give you an opportunity you wouldn't have otherwise to have your voice heard and to have your opinion matter.

While your parents are trying to support themselves, it's likely that you will have more time alone, whether that time is outside and around town or in your house. You can learn to cook. You can learn to use public transportation. You can learn how to do laundry and run a house. It's a few steps closer to living life like an adult.

Some people observe that children from divorced families are often more independent and responsible than children from stable marriages.

I'll let you in on a little secret: most kids have no idea how to do any of these things. And I'm not just talking about eight-year-old kids. I'm talking about eighteen-year-old kids too. In fact, there are plenty of adults who can't figure this stuff out because they never learned it when they were young. Speaking from personal experience, it's a really nice thing to be able to take care of yourself and not to have to depend on anyone else.

Two things come from independence: freedom and responsibility. It takes a lot of kids a long time to be able to handle those things. For you, if you are up to the challenge, you'll be years ahead of your peers. Who doesn't like a head start?

You Will Learn How to Fly

When I went to boarding school, I was sixteen. I got off a plane with lots of other kids, and half of them were freaking out. Their moms had packed their luggage; they didn't know where to pick it up or what to do. They had never flown alone. In all likelihood, you probably won't choose to go to boarding school, and you may never even have to travel by yourself until you've graduated from high school. But if you do, consider yourself lucky, and use it as an opportunity to get a leg up on people who don't know how to travel alone.

It's nice to be able to fly and get around on your own. It makes everything much easier. As the child of divorced parents, you'll learn fast how to pack your own bags and how to choose your own flights. The more responsibility you take on for yourself, the easier it all gets.

You Will Meet a Lot of New People

Stepparents. Stepcousins. Stepaunts and stepuncles. New friends, new neighbors, strangers on airplanes. Suddenly, you'll find that the circle of people you knew when your parents were together has grown exponentially. The benefits that come with meeting new people are too numerous to name, but I'll give it a shot.

Thanks to my ever-extending network of family and friends, I have contacts in hundreds of places around the world. My grandmother lives in Las Vegas. My stepgrandmother lives in L.A. I have stepcousins in Toronto. My brother's mother has a brother in Paris. My stepfather has friends in London. I have a second cousin in Florida, and more family in Baltimore, Seattle, Washington D.C., New York, Ohio, and Texas. It's reassuring and makes life easier to have safety and support nets of family and friends all over the world, in places I've never even been yet. All these people from all over the world can open your eyes

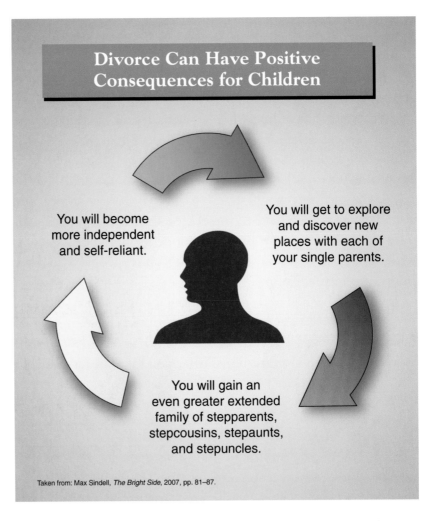

Divorce Can Have Positive Consequences for Children

You will become more independent and self-reliant.

You will get to explore and discover new places with each of your single parents.

You will gain an even greater extended family of stepparents, stepcousins, stepaunts, and stepuncles.

Taken from: Max Sindell, *The Bright Side*, 2007, pp. 81–87.

to new cultures and ways of life, and you'll find yourself knowing a lot more about the world than many of your peers who've never lived in a different city. With all these new people you can connect to, who knows where you'll find your next relative? You may have the opportunity to visit any number of places in the world, and even have someone with whom you can stay.

You Can Become a Resource

Your mission, should you choose to accept it, is to help other kids through this stuff too. Thousands of marriages end every day, and a lot of those marriages involve kids just like you, and just like me. You know them. They're in your classes at school, they attend your church or synagogue. You play soccer or baseball with them. A lot of them have no idea how to deal with it. They're looking for someone to talk to, and more than anything, they need someone who understands.

I was lucky. My parents and lots of people around me helped me figure a lot of this out, and I found help when I was young. You have this book, and chances are your parents are helping you a lot too. But many of these kids don't have this book, and their parents aren't helping them the same way. It's for kids like these that divorce really does become the worst thing that's ever happened in their lives. So if you want to, you can help. Find them, talk to them. A lot of kids might not want to talk about it, and you shouldn't force anyone to. I wouldn't want you to go around seeking out kids going through difficult divorces and demand that they share their life story with you—but if it comes up, then you're going to have a lot of useful things to tell them and advice to give.

Tell them that seeing a counselor isn't lame or useless. Explain that they aren't alone in this, and that it's not the end of the world, but rather a whole new set of opportunities to take advantage of. Remember, though, that you might end up hearing something bigger than you can handle, and it's up to you to use that information wisely. You don't want to betray anyone's trust, but if there is the potential for real danger, physical or otherwise, then you have a responsibility to make sure that person is safe. So don't try to save the world, but at least make it clear, if you want to, that you can offer a helping hand. Make yourself a new friend, and help someone. They'll thank you for it.

You Will Gain Insight

While watching my parents get divorced, I realized: This is the last thing I want to do when I grow up. I observed as my parents, two people who'd loved each other enough to raise me and stay married for ten years, had their marriage disintegrate into screaming matches and custody battles. I asked myself over and over again: How could this have happened? How could these two people who loved each other suddenly stop?

Ever since then, I've tried to figure out what makes a successful relationship work and what makes a successful relationship fall apart. I look at my parents to see what it was in each other that drove them apart. Sometimes I find personality traits in my parents that I don't like, which is never fun, but from that point on I do my best to never act in the same way. Watching my parents' divorce and subsequent remarriages, it seems that some of the most essential qualities for a successful relationship include complete trust, totally open and honest communication, and a willingness to listen and compromise. While getting married is easy, and staying married isn't much harder, staying married *and happy* seems to be all too rare these days. Perhaps the best thing that a divorce can teach you is more about who you are and about the reasons a relationship can either work or fall apart.

FIVE

A Stable Environment Following Divorce Has a Lifelong Impact on Children

Ohio State University

> In the following article, "After Divorce, Stable Families Help Minimize Long-Term Harm to Children," Ohio State University seeks to explain the findings of a recent study, "Stable Postdivorce Family Structures During Late Adolescence and Socioeconomic Consequences in Adulthood." The study, coauthored by associate professor of sociology Yongmin Sun, illustrates that a stable environment following divorce produces better social, educational, and economic outcomes for children in adulthood.

For children of divorce, what happens after their parents split up may be just as important to their long-term well-being as the divorce itself.

A new study found that children who lived in unstable family situations after their parents divorced fared much worse as adults on a variety of measures compared to children who had stable post-divorce family situations.

"For many children with divorced parents, particularly young ones, the divorce does not mark the end of family structure

Ohio State University, "After Divorce, Stable Families Help Minimize Long-Term Harm to Children," Ascribe Higher Education News Service, May 7, 2008. Reproduced by permission.

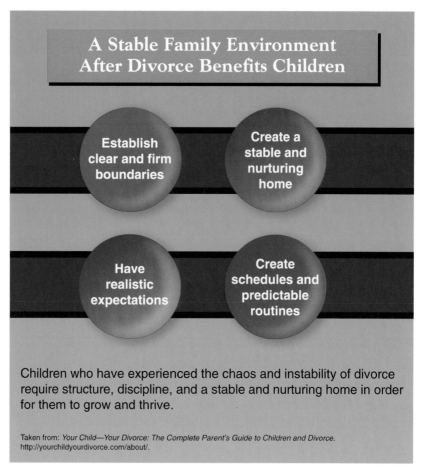

A Stable Family Environment After Divorce Benefits Children

Establish clear and firm boundaries

Create a stable and nurturing home

Have realistic expectations

Create schedules and predictable routines

Children who have experienced the chaos and instability of divorce require structure, discipline, and a stable and nurturing home in order for them to grow and thrive.

Taken from: *Your Child—Your Divorce: The Complete Parent's Guide to Children and Divorce.* http://yourchildyourdivorce.com/about/.

changes—it marks the beginning," said Yongmin Sun, co-author of the study and associate professor of sociology at Ohio State University's Mansfield campus.

"A stable family situation after divorce does not erase the negative effects of a divorce, but children in this situation fare much better than do those who experience chronic instability."

The study appears in a recent issue of the *Journal of Marriage and Family*. Sun conducted the study with Yuanzhang Li of the Allied Technology Group.

Data from Which Study Compiled

Data for this study came from the National Education Longitudinal Study, which surveyed thousands of students across the country beginning in 8th grade in 1988, when they were about 14 years old. They were surveyed again in 1990, 1992 and then again in 2000 when they were about 26 years old.

The study compared children who grew up in three different situations:

- Children who grew up in always-married households (5,303 children).
- Children whose parents divorced before the study began, but who lived in a stable family structure between ages 14 and 18 (954 children).
- Children whose parents divorced prior to the beginning of the study, and whose family situation changed once or twice between ages 14 and 18 (697 children).

In the two divorced family groups, children may have lived in single-parent families or ones with a stepparent. The key for this research was whether that arrangement—whichever it was—changed between ages 14 and 18.

The researchers compared how children in these groups fared on measures of education, income and poverty in 2000 when they were 26.

Stable Post-Divorce Environment Better for Children's Future

Results showed that young adults who grew up in stable post-divorce families had similar chances of attending college and living in poverty compared to those from always married families. But they fared less well on measures of the highest degree obtained, occupational prestige and income.

However, the young adults who lived in unstable family situations after their parents divorced did worse on all measures. In fact, they fared more than twice as poorly on most measures compared to their peers who had stable family situations.

For example, adults from stable post-divorce families earned about $1,800 a year less than similar adults from always-married families. But those adults whose family situations changed one or more times between ages 14 and 18 earned about $4,600 less.

Sun noted that some of the children in the unstable family group also underwent a custody change between ages 14 and 18. An analysis showed that they did not fare significantly differently from those who were in unstable families, but did not experience a custody change.

There were also no significant differences between how boys and girls responded to family stability after a divorce, Sun said.

Why do children of divorce fare less well than those who grew up with parents who stayed married?

Economic and Social Resources Influence Well-Being

This study found that for those in stable post-divorce families, the difference in adult well-being was mostly due to a shortage of economic and social resources. Compared to always-married parents, divorced parents had a lower level of income, didn't talk to their children as much about school-related matters, had

Research has shown that a stable postdivorce family environment allows children to focus on their own needs rather than on a continuing family crisis.

fewer interactions with other parents, and moved their children to new schools more often.

"As many previous divorce studies point out, divorce reduces social resources within families because children have fewer interactions with the non-custodial parent, and in many cases, don't get the quantity and quality of parenting from the custodial parent," Sun said.

"In addition, after a family disruption, parents may not invest as much time with teachers and other parents in the community, all of which lead to a lower level of child well-being."

For children in unstable families, the decline in social and economic resources was only part of the reason for the shortfalls they experienced in adulthood.

"These children probably experience a lot of stress and disruption from sources that we didn't measure in this study," he said.

Stabilized Environment Following Divorce Clearly Beneficial

These findings provide a clear message about how parents who are divorcing can best help their children, Sun said.

"A stabilized post-divorce family environment is clearly helpful for children, particularly for adolescents, such as those we studied, because stability allows children to focus on their own developmental needs rather than on continual family crises," he said.

The study was supported by grants from the Ohio State University Initiative in Population Research and a population research center grant awarded by the National Institute of Child Health and Human Development.

SIX

Divorced Parents' Varied Values and Beliefs Benefit Children

Ruth Bettelheim

Ruth Bettelheim has been a practicing psychotherapist, marriage and family counselor, and lecturer for over forty years and has taught courses on child development at the Claremont Graduate School and the California School for Professional Psychology. In the essay below Bettelheim asserts that despite the challenges children face in living in postdivorce families, these experiences provide them with opportunities to develop skills that foster adaptability, courtesy, and cooperation. Children, for example, are required to confront the reality that in a binuclear family there is no one right way to do things. This requires, she argues, that children adapt to different situations, understanding that what one parent believes and adheres to may be completely opposite to what their other parent believes and values. In order to get along and not offend their parents or stepparents, Bettelheim argues that children are forced to learn quickly what the rules are and act accordingly. As a result, children become particularly adroit in discerning risks and dangers in new situations. In addition, she claims that living in two separate and

Ruth Bettelheim, "Binuclear Family," *Greater Good*, vol. 4, Fall 2007, pp. 1–6. Reproduced by permission of the publisher and author.

distinct households challenges children to become in-dependent thinkers. Faced with opposing viewpoints, children have to weigh the differences, then arrive at their own conclusions based on what they believe is right. It is these very skills, she argues, that stand them in good stead as they venture out into the world.

I remember the scene in my house on a Friday afternoon, two years after my divorce. My son comes home from school, his temper already short because of the coming transition: My ex-husband is picking up the children to take them to his house for the weekend. My son remembers to pack his backpack and then has time to play a video game. His sister, four years younger, does not remember. She is deeply engaged with her Barbies. Suddenly, the doorbell rings: Dad has arrived, and he wants to leave immediately to avoid the rush-hour traffic.

Living in a Binuclear Family Fosters Good Social Skills

My daughter must stuff her bag as quickly as she can while her brother rushes to the door, not wanting to displease his father. He yells at his sister to hurry up! as she struggles to remember what she needs. I come in to say goodbye and give each of them a hug. Meanwhile, both children know that Dad is waiting. They want to get out the door as quickly as possible, but they do not want to slight my feelings. And they cannot afford to leave anything behind that they might need for school on Monday. My son hugs me and dashes to the car—my daughter clings to me a few moments longer, filled with conflicting feelings, before running after her brother.

Both children are under pressure, caught by opposing loyalties. They long to please both parents, and they have to remember every single thing they will need for the three days they are spending with their father. This is emotionally charged multitasking of the most demanding sort, repeated twice a week with each transfer from one parent's house to the other's.

Walking on a Narrow Bridge

My son describes his life immediately prior to and after the divorce as walking on a narrow bridge across the sea. The tides—his parents' moods, needs, and desires, and the tensions and conflicts between them—threatened to pull him down and drown him on either side. My daughter describes it as being put on trial in a foreign country where she knew neither the laws nor the language. Both children needed to become exquisitely aware of what each of their parents was feeling, how each of us would react to things said or done, in order to protect themselves from feeling emotionally swamped or from being barred from a desired activity, such as guitar lessons or a trip to the beach. As a result, they became highly intuitive observers of others' emotions and superb diplomats, able to soothe the most fraught situations. They learned these skills both out of self-protection and out of loyalty to both parents. And they are not alone.

Study after study, even those conducted by the most vocal critics of divorce, has found that adult children of divorce are more empathic than their peers and have a greater devotion to honesty, kindness, integrity, and compassion in relationships. Although it may seem counterintuitive, the great challenges they face present these children with powerful opportunities for growth.

Living through a divorce is almost always difficult for children, but if it unfolds in a way that makes them feel empowered, the next time they face something hard or unfamiliar they will be able to do so with confidence rather than fear. As Judith Wallerstein writes in *The Unexpected Legacy of Divorce*:

> Many children of divorce are stronger for their struggles. They think of themselves as survivors who have learned to rely on their own judgment and to take responsibility for themselves and others at a young age. They have had to invent their own morality and values. They understand the importance of economic independence and hard work. They do not take relationships lightly. Most maintain reverence for good family life.

Although this process is often painful for children, and although it is natural for us to regret their suffering, it is also unjust to the children of divorce to remain blind to what they have gained.

Discussions of divorce rarely consider these complexities. Instead, the last two decades have produced a tidal wave of divorce hysteria, and many divorced parents feel deeply stigmatized and guilty as a result. Divorce is blamed for the troubles of young people; the feeling is that if the youth of today is "in crisis," this must, at least in part, have to do with the ravages of growing up in a nontraditional family, without the benefit of traditional parental roles. . . .

Two Sets of Rules

After a divorce, children no longer live in a world where there is one agreed-upon set of rules, values, or beliefs. Suddenly there are two sets of rules about bedtime, bath time, homework, TV,

Postdivorce children often have to deal with two sets of rules for homework, bedtime, TV watching, and what constitutes good and bad behavior.

movies, video games, hugs, table manners, good behavior, and bad behavior. In one house you must attend church; in the other religion is disregarded. In one you must always say please, thank you, hello, goodbye, and ask permission to go out; in the other these things are not necessary. In one house it is a sign of being a " goody-two-shoes" to worry about arriving to school on time and getting each assignment in promptly, while in the other these are required. The two homes are in fact two different cultures, and because of this, children in "binuclear" post-divorce families become adept at living in two worlds. They are forced to recognize that there is more than one right way to do things and that they had better learn very quickly what the rules are in each milieu so that they don't upset either parent or get into trouble.

I remember my son as a 13-year-old, my daughter as a fourth grader. They were faced with conflicts of loyalty that permeated their lives on a daily basis. My daughter expressed her anxiety by withdrawing into herself, attempting to placate the powers in her life through accommodation, whereas my son shifted the focus through rambunctious or irritable behavior. They both did the best they could. When businessmen travel, they receive guides to the basic rules of behavior in each culture they visit. Children do not. They must figure it out themselves, and frequently the adults in their lives deny that such a problem even exists.

Despite these challenges, if attentive parents skillfully negotiate it, the experience of living in two family cultures can teach children important skills. Interestingly, these skills encompass both traditionally "masculine" and "feminine" attributes. Both boys and girls in post-divorce families must learn to be diplomatic, sensitive to others' needs, persuasive, empathic, nurturing, multitasking, resilient in new situations, independent, self-confident, and self-aware. For my children, both now successful adults, it means they like living abroad from time to time and enjoy traveling. They have no trouble adapting to new cultures, whether at college or at the in-laws' house, abroad or in the workplace. They quickly and easily adjust to new jobs, with different demands and workplace environments. It is second nature to them to quickly read and assess new situations, figure out how they work, and how to become valued assets in them. They take moving across the country, or the globe, in stride, and their friends often turn to them when in need of emotional insight and support. Like so many other children of divorce, they are succeeding where our culture expects them to fail.

Additionally, in my experience and in that of researchers across the ideological spectrum, living in two divergent cultures causes children to become self-reflective and autonomous thinkers. Each parent's point of view must be considered and evaluated, though they are often at odds with each other. As a result, children quickly learn that there are at least two valid points of view on almost every issue, and it is up to him or her to decide which ones make the most sense. Such children are forced to develop ethics and opinions of their own, based on their own perceptions and experiences. In the same way, in each household these children are likely to be viewed and evaluated in dissimilar ways, since each parent values traits differently. As a result, they cannot fully accept the self-image imposed on them by either parent, but instead must develop a sense of identity that is uniquely their own. . . .

Challenges for Parents

Researchers of all stripes have found that most, if not all, of the problems blamed on divorce (other than those caused by poverty) are actually attributable to a lack of warm, consistent, attentive, authoritative, and respectful parenting. In order to maintain children's self-confidence and teach them the self-control that they need to thrive, parents must set and enforce boundaries; this is particularly true for boys, who often have greater difficulty learning self-regulation than girls. It is self-control and self-confidence that enable children to make use of the skills they learn in a binuclear family.

Many post-divorce families have been paralyzed by parents' negative assumptions about divorce and their feelings of guilt. It is not that they are wrong to believe that divorce has been a painful experience: Divorce is difficult for most, if not all, children. The problem is that these parents sometimes forget what their children need. For in many ways, children in divorced families need the same things as children in every other kind of family: love, structure, consistent and reasonable boundaries, and for their parents to believe that they are not damaged individuals. As Mavis Hetherington, the author of the largest longitudinal study ever conducted on children in divorced families, points out in her book *For Better or for Worse: Divorce Reconsidered*:

> Coping with the challenges of divorce and life in a single-parent family seems actually to enhance the ability of some children to deal with future stresses. But children can't cope alone; there needs to be a supportive adult in their lives to help buffer them from adversity. . . .

What matters is that children know that someone cares about and respects them enough to pay attention to their behavior and to set boundaries that protect their well-being and development.

Given the right sort of parenting, children who grow up in binuclear families gain a unique opportunity. Our society is changing at an ever-accelerating pace, and we now live in a global service economy. Many have documented the attributes needed to excel in such a society; borrowing from the work of psychologist and cultural commentator Daniel Goleman, these traits include empathy, emotional awareness, self-confidence, self-control, social deftness, persuasiveness, resilience, cooperation, and adaptability.

This list of traits closely matches those learned by children of both genders growing up in binuclear families, especially those fortunate enough to have caring, authoritative parents. Given the premium on these abilities, children from binuclear families may actually be at an advantage later in life. They will have been forced to develop a skill set that will enable them to be uniquely competent partners, parents, and professionals. Their futures can be bright—not in spite of but because of what they have endured.

SEVEN

Custody Laws Violate Parental Rights

Stephen Baskerville

In the following article, "How to Turn a Free People into Slaves," author Stephen Baskerville argues that although divorce itself is an egregious act, it is the power of the government to resolve custody issues that is even more precarious. He asserts that while marriage is a contract entered into by two people, the government can, when a woman decides to divorce her husband, forcibly use its power to separate a man from all his possessions, including his children. Baskerville asserts that even if a father considers his home common property and therefore has the right to stay in that common home and care for his children, the government can use its coercive power to restrict what he can and cannot do. He argues that once couples divorce, the government assumes authority over their children through mandated custody agreements.

Baskerville holds a PhD from the London School of Economics and is president of the American Coalition for Fathers and Children and assistant professor of government at Patrick Henry College. He has written many books, the latest of which is *Taken into Custody: The War Against Fathers, Marriage, and the Family* (Cumberland House, 2007).

A commonplace of the American Revolution held that citizens must have a love for liberty and a willingness to sacrifice and fight for it. Otherwise, no paper constitution alone can ever preserve their freedom.

Today, it is becoming equally commonplace that this spirit of liberty is leaving Americans, that we are becoming "a nation of sheep," as Judge Andrew Napolitano puts it in a new book, who acquiesce in the progressive abrogation of our Constitution and liberty.

This is plausibly attributed to several factors: mass affluence, cultural decadence, the loss of religious faith. But I believe one major factor has been seriously overlooked: the breakdown of the family and the growth of divorce. Moreover, this is not some nebulous "cultural" contributor that somehow saps Americans' willingness to defend their freedom. The cause-and-effect is directly demonstrable. The reason is that we are now raising our children according to the principles of tyranny.

Divorce sends many harmful messages to children and future citizens: that we can break vows we make to God and others; that family members may be discarded at will. But among the most destructive are about the role of government: that government is their de facto parent that may exercise unlimited power (including remove and criminalize their real parent) merely by claiming to act for their greater good.

While feminists push divorce-on-demand as a "civil liberty," in practice divorce has become our society's most authoritarian institution.

Government Uses Coercive Power to Restrict What Spouses Can or Cannot Do

Some 80% of divorces are unilateral: the action of one spouse alone and over the objection of the other. One spouse's "freedom" to leave a freely contracted marriage, therefore, means tyranny over the other spouse in forcibly separating him from his home, property, and most seriously, his children. And while marriage is an agreement freely entered into by both parties, with only a nominal role for the government, unilateral divorce must be enforced by the coercive machinery of the state. Otherwise, the involuntary divorced spouse may continue to claim the right to live in the common home, to enjoy the common property, and above all, to parent the common children. These must be curtailed, or at least controlled, by the state.

This entails a massive extension of government power—and straight into precisely the realm from which its exclusion until now virtually defines freedom and limited government: the realm of private life.

The moment either spouse files for divorce, even if the other is legally unimpeachable, the government takes control of the children, who become effectively wards of the state. Unauthorized contact by a parent becomes a crime, and the excluded parent can be arrested and incarcerated without trial through a variety of other means that by-pass constitutional due process protections: domestic violence accusations, child abuse accusations, inability to pay "child support," even inability to pay attorneys' fees.

Legal jargon and clichés like "divorce," "custody battle," and "child support" have led Americans to acquiesce in this massive intrusion of state power over their freedom. We don't say that the government arbitrarily took away someone's children; we say he "lost custody." We don't say a legally innocent citizen was interrogated by government agents over how he lives his private life; we say there was a "custody battle." We don't say a citizen was incarcerated without trial or charge for debt he could not possibly pay and did nothing to incur; we say he "didn't pay his child support." These clichés and jargon inure us to tyranny.

The Effect of Government Rules on Children

But worst of all, we are raising generations of children to believe that police and jails exist not to protect us from dangerous criminals but to keep away one of their parents, and that the criminal justice apparatus may be marshaled against family members who have committed no legal infraction.

Some contend that the message children receive in custody battles is that the state functions as a dictatorship, employing an arbitrary use of power against one parent.

Using instruments of public criminal justice to punish private hurts turns the family into government-occupied territory. The children experience family life not as a place of love, cooperation, compromise, trust, and forgiveness. Instead they receive a firsthand lesson in tyranny. Empowered by the state and functioning essentially as a government official, the custodial parent can issue orders to the non-custodial parent, undermine his authority with the children, dictate the terms of his access to them, talk to and about him contemptuously and condescendingly in the presence of the children as if he were himself a naughty child—all with the backing of state officials.

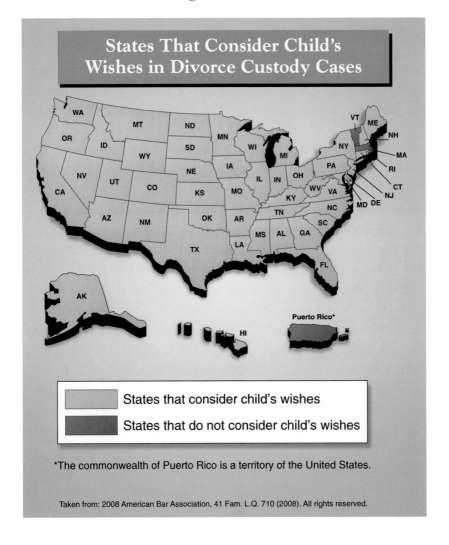

States That Consider Child's Wishes in Divorce Custody Cases

States that consider child's wishes

States that do not consider child's wishes

*The commonwealth of Puerto Rico is a territory of the United States.

Eventually the children understand that the force keeping away one of their parents is the police, who are the guarantors of the custodial parent's supremacy. Thus the message the children receive about both the family and the state is that they are dictatorships, ruled by an arbitrary power which can be marshaled against private enemies and even family members for personal grievances. If a loved one disagrees with us or hurts our feelings or is simply no longer desired, there is no need for forgiveness because a telephone call will have him removed, and the police will make sure he stays away. And if the police can be used to arrest Dad because he does something Mom doesn't like, what will they do to me if I do something Mom doesn't like?

Implications of Government's Heavy Hand

After witnessing this dictatorship over the non-custodial parent, the children may then experience it themselves. Lacking firm authority that is in any sense moral, as well as any effective restraints on her behavior, the custodial parent now exercises unchecked power over the children as well, a relationship that becomes increasingly strained and acrimonious as the children grow older, less credulous, and more rebellious. As the children react adversely to this destruction of their home and father, or as the cute and cuddly children become rebellious adolescents, they can be turned over to state agencies by their mothers, as large numbers now are. If more vigorous instruments are required, various arms of the state—psychotherapists, police, and penal institutions—can be marshaled against the children as well. Thus the drugging and institutionalization of children in foster care, psychiatric hospitals, juvenile detention facilities, and jails that has become increasingly familiar.

In July 2001, the *Progressive* magazine detailed how "parents" are now turning their troublesome teenagers whom they cannot control over to the police. Overwhelmingly, though the politically correct article does not point this out, these parents are single mothers. In the single-mother home, "Wait till your father gets home," has been replaced by, "I can turn you over to Social Services."

On the other hand, perhaps someday they can commandeer the police and jails against family members with whom they have differences or against anyone who hurts their feelings. While many children are materially impoverished by family breakdown, in other cases the systematic bribery dispensed by the divorce industry extends to the children themselves, who may be rewarded for their cooperation with material opulence, forcibly extracted from their father and used to corrupt his children and give them too a stake in his plunder and exile.

Government Control Is Reminiscent of Earlier Times

It is not difficult to see that this is a highly unhealthy system to have in a free society. In fact, the logic is reminiscent of another system of domestic dictatorship that once tried unsuccessfully to co-exist with free civil government. Politically, the most powerful argument against slavery—and what eventually did more than any other to bring about the realization of how threatening it was to democratic freedom—was less its physical cruelty than its moral degeneracy: the tyrannical habits it encouraged in the slaveholder, the servile ones it fostered in the slave, and the moral degradation it engendered in both. Such dispositions were said to be incompatible with the kind of republican virtue required for free self-government.

Abolitionist Charles Sumner's warning of slavery's impact on the moral development of white children growing up in slave societies was at least as alarming as concerns about cruelty to black ones. "Their hearts, while yet tender with childhood, are necessarily hardened by this conduct, and their subsequent lives perhaps bear enduring testimony to this legalized uncharitableness," he wrote. "They are unable to eradicate it from their natures. . . . Their characters are debased, and they become less fit for the magnanimous duties of a good citizen." Something similar may be seen today in the children of the divorce regime. No people can remain free who harbor within themselves a system of dictatorship or raise their children according to its principles.

EIGHT

Flexibility in Custody Helps Children Adjust to Divorce

Constance Ahrons

In the following excerpt from her book *We're Still Family*, Constance Ahrons argues that in a divorce, children and money become the issues over which parents seek to win control and power. As a result, deciding where the children are going to live might become a contentious issue. She claims that while many parents seek to avoid these conflicts, many do not. In these instances, counselors and therapists play an important role in clarifying when issues of power prevent parents from making good decisions. Custody arrangements, she adds, should be made in the best interest of the child. If custody remains unresolved, the parents' indecision gives the courts permission to decide the fate of their children. This can be a worst-case scenario for all involved, she concludes.

Ahrons is professor emerita of Sociology and former director of the Marriage and Family Therapy Doctoral Training Program at the University of Southern California. A senior scholar and founding cochair of the Council on Contemporary Families, she is an internationally renowned lecturer, consultant, and workshop leader. Ahrons is director of Divorce and Marriage Consulting

Constance Ahrons, *We're Still Family: What Grown Children Have to Say About Their Parents' Divorce.* New York: HarperCollins, 2004. Copyright © 2004 by Constance Ahrons, Ph.D. Granted by permission of the author and the Sandra Dijkstra Literary Agency.

Associates in San Diego, California. She has authored many books, which include *The Good Divorce*, and coauthored *Divorced Families*.

E ven though more than one million parents divorce every year, most parents feel they have stepped into uncharted territory as they try to meet the needs of their family. Second only to agonizing over the actual decision to divorce, deciding where the children will live and how they will have time with both parents is the most difficult and painful decision parents have to make. It directly confronts the harsh reality that divorce will change everyone's daily lives.

One given is that *all* living arrangements fall short of the ideal. Another is that parents often disagree. They may agree that they want to have living arrangements that permit them to continue to share parenting, but how they accomplish this across two households without clear-cut guidelines is no simple task. Even in the best of situations, the decisions that parents need to make about custody and living arrangements are ambiguous, complex and often painful.

To the stresses of the daily practicalities such as child care, housing and financial concerns, add the strong emotions they each have about ending their marriage. Then layer this with their concerns about the children's welfare and the importance of their relationships with their children. It's a rare parent who doesn't feel overwhelmed. Although it certainly can't resolve all the issues of this difficult decision, listening to the views of the grown children will provide some guidelines for determining optimal living situations. . . .

Fighting for Control

The overriding factor in the living arrangement equation is the relationship between the parents. Practicalities of schedules become intertwined with feelings of sadness and anger and fears about loss. Married parents have the freedom to decide how involved they

Divorced couples often put their children into the middle of divorce proceedings by using them to get revenge against the other parent.

want to be in their children's daily lives, but as divorce looms, worry creeps in about whether and how they will be able to continue their involvement.

We must also remember that, although assigning fault is no longer a necessary *legal* component of divorce, this does not settle the *emotional* need to find fault. As you think about and tell your personal account of why your marriage is ending, there is often a need to locate a cause, and that cause is often labeled as "your spouse's fault." Once fault is assigned, of course, the perpetrator needs to be punished. In a marriage, if a spouse is angry, there are usually many small ways to punish the other, such as withdrawing or withholding affection, sex or money. But once the divorce decision has been made, the major avenues of inflicting punishment are the children and money. When divorcing couples are in the grip of issues of power and control over these two most important resources, working out living arrangements often becomes more about winning than best interests.

Fortunately, many parents are able to avoid these kinds of power struggles. But for those who can't, there are mediators, counselors, therapists, lawyers, court-affiliated professionals and judges who can help clarify when personal power struggles are preventing the making of good decisions. And it is important to remember that, although living and child-care arrangements need to be decided at the time new households are established, they can be renegotiated as lives change and personal angers subside.

Clearly, deciding children's living arrangements is extraordinarily complex. It is almost always an interplay between emotional factors, practical factors and legal issues that has its roots in societal views about gender, parenting and divorce.

What Custody Means

First, let's take a brief look at the concept of *custody*, which is the term for who will be legally responsible for the children, financially, emotionally and physically. Custody often has little to do with how living arrangements actually get worked out. In fact, most of the adult children in our study didn't even know

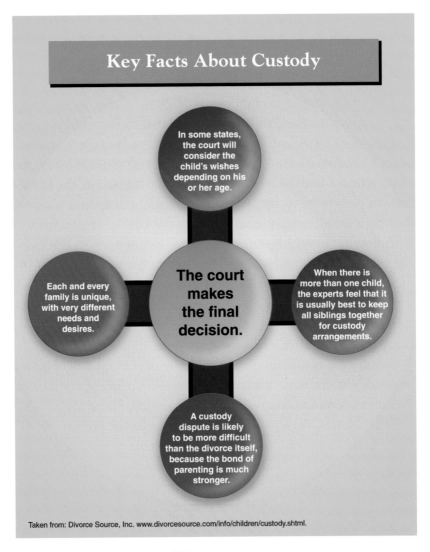

Key Facts About Custody

In some states, the court will consider the child's wishes depending on his or her age.

Each and every family is unique, with very different needs and desires.

The court makes the final decision.

When there is more than one child, the experts feel that it is usually best to keep all siblings together for custody arrangements.

A custody dispute is likely to be more difficult than the divorce itself, because the bond of parenting is much stronger.

Taken from: Divorce Source, Inc. www.divorcesource.com/info/children/custody.shtml.

what their family's legal custody arrangement was. It was only in those families where parents continued to battle over custody that children were aware of the precise ruling.

Many courts and professionals today are seeking to replace the language of custody and visitation with language more appropriate to the times: In place of the word "custody," they are using terms such as "allocation of child-rearing responsibilities," "living arrangements" and "parenting plans." When allocating parental responsibilities, the courts will now use such terms as "in-home parent" and "residential parent" (as opposed to custodial and noncustodial parent), terms that can be applied to either parent during the time when children are in their care. Acknowledging that legal joint custody is more a concept of parental "rights" than it is a designation of responsibilities, parenting plans are now incorporated as part of the final divorce decree. These plans spell out the specifics of living arrangements and parental responsibilities.

Because custody legislation differs from state to state, this new language and approach is not consistently applied. But this new direction reduces the ambiguity and helps parents think through and work out the nitty-gritty specifics of how they continue to responsibly parent their children across households.

How Parents Make Custody Decisions

Ideally, custody decisions are thought to be based on "the best interests of the child." However, although much has been written on the subject, there are no hard-and-fast rules about how to define "best interests." In custody disputes, such criteria as the child's relationship with each parent and which parent is to be the primary caretaker are agreed upon by most professionals, but the realities of what is in the best interests of *your* child are not easily derived from any standardized list.

Who decides what is in a child's best interests? Ideally, of course, his or her parents. But divorcing parents are likely to have different opinions. You may feel that it's best for your children to live with you because you have been the primary parent, the parent who did most of the child care. Or you may feel that your child should live with you because you are the better disciplinarian or can afford to keep and maintain the family home. Maybe one of you questions the other's parenting abilities or feels that you have a closer relationship with the child.

Here's a typical route to deciding custody. If you are in conflict over the decision, you decide to seek the advice of a professional. But you soon find out that even experts may differ about which custody arrangement is best for your child. One expert believes that one stable home is most important; another believes that spending equal time with both parents is most important. If you still can't resolve the custody conflicts, even after you've consulted the experts, by default you decide to let the court decide. If you go this route you and all your children will then be required to have psychological evaluations and perhaps you will each hire your own psychologists to testify on your behalf. Then you sadly discover that how the custody decision will be made rests not on some agreed-upon policies but by the judge who hears your case. So you listen to your friends, your lawyers, your therapists or your mediators tell you how the judge is *likely* to decide and you realize that you are caught in a confusing maze that doesn't seem to make any rational sense at all. . . .

Conclusions

Regardless of the living arrangement, children seem to get most upset when they are forced to be go-betweens. Carrying information back and forth between parents makes them feel disloyal to one parent or the other. They want their parents to pay attention to their feelings and then try to resolve the problems that are making the situations stressful.

Parents want to move on with their individual lives after divorce and often this involves changing jobs and changing residences, and children rarely like such changes.

If parents are unable to contain their conflicts on their own, then they need to seek out professionals who can help. There are many sources of help available, such as counselors and mediators. Now, in many states, there are special masters, experienced professionals who can help parents with their decisions, and parenting coordinators and consultants who are specifically trained to help divorced parents work together for the sake of their children. These professionals help parents set appropriate boundaries and mutually plan and coordinate arrangements that give priority to their children's needs. It's been more or less the norm that living arrangements remain fixed while children's developmental needs change. It is encouraging to see that many parenting plans now include planned negotiations for change.

These plans note specifically that as children's developmental needs change the plans need to be reviewed and, if necessary, also changed. This is difficult for most parents but it is absolutely necessary for children. Even though joint legal custody has now become the norm, there is still much controversy over shared parenting. Although child development experts may differ, most consider that children's ages, their temperaments, their emotional ties and attachment to each parent and the ability of each parent to provide a nurturing, consistent and stable home are important factors in determining how to formulate living arrangements.

Some experts believe that children need the stability of a primary home. Although I certainly agree that stability is important to children, I don't believe it should be equated with a single home. Most important, children need the stability of maintaining meaningful relationships with their parents and extended family. They also need the stability of knowing that they will be safe and secure. Parents who keep their children's needs for stability as their primary focus can settle on living arrangements that make it possible for children to spend time with them both. As these adult children have shown us, there are no hard-and-fast rules about how much time works best. It boils down to how parents relate and communicate with each other, how competent and caring each parent is, and how each child relates to each parent. Many parents can make these decisions amicably, and when they do they usually work out well for the children. For those who can't, there are now many resources available to help them.

Today the courts and state legislatures are openly debating "What's in the best interests of the children?" Although we certainly don't have all the answers, the fact that we are asking the important questions is hopeful. If parents are in conflict, will the children benefit or be harmed from shared living arrangements? Should the courts be able to order joint physical custody when parents are in a legal battle because each wants sole custody? What to do when parents do not live near each other geographically? And further, what to do when parents who do live near one another are sharing living arrangements and one parent decides to relocate?

The point is, there is no one-size-fits-all answer; temperament, age, relationships with each parent, sibling relationships, the relationship between parents, and parents' remarriages all combine in different permutations to create different outcomes as far as living arrangements go. But for the most part, children want to spend time with both parents, and for them the keys to making shared parenting work seem to be *flexibility* that takes their unique needs and particular parental relationships into account, *geographical proximity* so they don't have to hassle with long trips, and most of all, *good communication between parents.*

The bottom line is: *When parents can cooperate, they can make most arrangements work.*

NINE

Divorce Harms the Relationship Between Adolescents and Fathers

Tracy Kendricks

In the following article, "Parenting: Dads and Teens Often Struggle with Their Relationship After the Divorce," excerpted below, Tracy Kendricks examines the impact of divorce on the father-child relationship. Citing research from Alan Booth's recent study, "Postdivorce Father-Adolescent Closeness," Kendricks argues that of all the relationships hurt by parental divorce, it is the father-child relationship that suffers the greatest impact. This is due in part, she argues, to the fact that it is the father who leaves the home following the divorce. His departure oftentimes lessens the degree to which he can see and interact with his children. In addition, Kendricks examines how the father-child relationship is further harmed by the anger that still exists between divorced couples. Left unresolved, these issues and conflicts can undermine any relationship a father may have with his children. Kendrick is a writer for divorce360.com, an Internet Web site that provides help, advice, and community for people contemplating, going through, or recovering from divorce and the issues around it.

D ivorce can strain relationships for years. But a team of researchers at Penn State University has found that divorce impacts different family relationships in different ways. The closeness between fathers and teens is harmed the most in a divorce.

Dr. Alan Booth, a professor of sociology and human development, co-authored the study. He found that divorced or not, there's a tendency for mothers to be more involved with children, especially teens. "Studies indicate that fathers are less involved. . . ," Dr. Booth reports. "We just don't have a heavy investment in the kids."

As kids grow, they tend to grow "away"—toward peers, school and the world. "The relationship with the father declines normally, just in the natural course of things," Booth says, adding that when parents divorce, "fathers are more likely to let it slide."

David Vendig, 43, is an exception. It's been two years since the father of three children (ages 13, 10, and 7) moved out of the Los Angeles home he shared with his ex-wife. And even though he moved just a few blocks away, it's not easy to parent post-divorce. Especially a teenager. "Finding alone time with any one of them takes planning and effort," Vendig says.

Another impediment is internal. "The other obstacle is self-doubt. Not knowing or believing that what I plan—or, if it's just hanging out—is good enough." Vendig's concerns are shared by many men. Dr. Booth says that's because mothers are more comfortable in the nurturing role.

Other Challenges Fathers Face

Whatever the circumstances, the Penn State study was clear: fathers and teens have a special set of challenges after divorce. The first is proximity. Dad is often the one who moves out, leaving the kids with the same schools, friends and address. But his time with the kids is cut down considerably. "It's just hard for dads to keep up," Dr. Booth found.

Also, Dad's new place is often not as comfortable—"I have a small apartment," Vendig says—and the kids aren't likely to feel

Because fathers are often the parent who moves out of the house, it is harder for them to find quality time with their children.

at home. In order to maintain the closeness they had before divorce, most fathers will have to increase their involvement with their kids. And that's something the majority of fathers just don't do, the study shows.

Then there's bad blood. The conflicts that cause a couple to divorce aren't resolved when the marriage ends. And that can be a big obstacle to dads maintaining relationships with their kids. Jane Reardon, M.A. MFT, a marriage and family therapist practicing in Los Angeles, says father-child relationships are vulnerable to anger between ex-spouses. "Mothers may find it impossible to contain the hurt rage they experience as a result of the change in their financial status and increased amount of responsibility for childrearing," she says.

Many women retaliate by badmouthing the ex-spouse, which can poison the children against him. But mothers are not alone in dealing with the fallout of the breakup. Either party's emotional residue can cast a shadow on the post-divorce relationship with the kids. Vendig explains it well. "If I am not careful about the contact I have with their mother—meaning if I let myself get too close—my feelings of hurt and anger come up and it keeps me from being present with the kids."

Divorce can affect the kids often decades into the future. In Reardon's practice, she sees clients—adults in their 20s and 30s—who are still dealing with the aftermath of their parents' battles. "They now feel fragmented in their recollections," Reardon says, "and as adults have a harder time claiming their identity and forming sustained intimate relationships."

Mothers Play an Important Role

That's just one reason to resolve the issues that led to the divorce—which Penn State researchers found yields a number of dividends, chiefly, her cooperation and support. "If he keeps mom happy, she'll be less resistant," Dr. Booth says. Often a mother is the deciding factor in whether, how often, or how much kids see their dad. "If the mother is supportive, she'll push from her end," Booth says.

Reardon sees the benefits: "My experience treating adult clients from divorced families shows a direct correlation between the continued involvement of both parents after the divorce, and the client's level of functioning." It's important to stay in front of your child's mind. Call the child regularly, send letters, send gifts. Continue to keep the child's attention. . . .

Impact of Relationships on Father-Child Closeness

A final obstacle pops up once the parents have moved on to a new relationship. As a psychologist, Reardon treats many children of divorced parents, now grown. She says her clients' biggest complaint "is when either parent attempted to integrate their children too quickly into their new relationship."

While divorced dads may be eager to rebuild a family with the new partner, "teenagers are typically resistant to the plan," Reardon says. They often respond by exercising the only power they have—refusing to visit. "Single parents need to be very mindful of their own agendas in trying to blend new families too quickly," Reardon advises. "The comfort level of the children needs to take precedence over the accommodation of a new partner."

Dads need to take into account the length of time the family has been separated, as well as the length of the new relationship. Dr. Booth believes the new relationships "have a tendency to take time and energy away from the kids" and men need to make sure they choose a new partner who is open to children. "It's important that he select a woman who likes kids and isn't opposed to being involved with a child." If a new girlfriend opposes a man's children, Dr. Booth observes, "it's very difficult for the dad to maintain close contact with them."

Fathers Have Some Control over Father-Child Relationships

The Penn State study did find some heartening news. For one thing, kids themselves can make a big difference in their relationship with their dad. "Kids have an effect on their fathers," Dr. Booth asserts. "If the kids want to maintain the relationship, they will." And that's something a dad can exert some control over. "It's important to stay at the front of your child's mind," urges Dr. Booth. "Call the child regularly, send letters, send gifts. Continue to keep the child's attention, even though the child may be mad that dad left."

It may take a while, even years, but Dr. Booth believes a father's actions over time do make an impression. "Eventually the child will see the dad differently, especially if the dad is really sincere."

Last but not least, divorce, say Penn State researchers, can also have the surprising effect of actually strengthening a dad's relationship with his teens—something Vendig is finding out first hand. "For me, processing this event has been a long growing process that includes stepping up as a father—probably more than anything else."

In Vendig's experience the key to staying close to his son is to accept the process as just that—something that gets easier over time. He urges dads to go easy on themselves. "Be kind to yourself as guilt and shame are bound to come up," he says. "It will be messy at times, but surrendering to it all can bring freedom. As a father, and as a man."

TEN

Divorced Mothers Can Harm Father-Child Relationships

Amy J.L. Baker

The term *parental alienation syndrome* has come to signify the conflict between parents, most often parents in divorce, in which one or more children align themselves with one parent in order to alienate the other. In the following excerpt from her work, *Adult Children of Parental Alienation Syndrome*, Amy J.L. Baker asserts that although incidents of parental alienation differ from one family to another, a similar pattern emerges among these differences. She argues that in her research, which covered fourteen families, the mother is the "custodial alienating parent," while the father is the "noncustodial targeted parent." In these instances, Baker argues, the mother has a "narcissistic personality disorder" in that she is completely self-absorbed and in constant need of attention. She is more concerned about having her own needs met than fulfilling the needs of her children. In addition, she does not see her children as individuals and has an unhealthy attachment to them. Baker argues that this personality disorder may well stimulate alienation. Baker concludes that because women feel especially vulnerable after divorce, they look to their children for support and encouragement. When children spend time with their father, the narcissistic mother considers this experience a deep loss. According to Baker, a mother's attempt to further alienate her children from their father is a way to counter that loss and anger. She adds that children may relinquish any rights to see their father simply to retain the love and approval of their mother.

E very story of parental alienation is somewhat different. Each person has his or her own individual voice and unique tale to tell. However, even among these disparate experiences, patterns can be detected. . . .

In [some] families the parents were divorced; the mother was the custodial alienating parent, and the father was the noncustodial targeted parent. The most distinguishing feature of these families was that the alienating mother appeared to have a narcissistic personality disorder. That is, she had a pervasive relational style that was selfish and grandiose with an inability to truly comprehend the needs and feelings of others. For example, Mitch described his mother as ". . . definitely totally conceited. She thought of herself as always wanting the best in things. She was very insistent about her skills and if somebody didn't recognize that, that was their problem not hers. Her actions were self-centered. She really did see herself as the center of the universe." Likewise, Nicole believed about her mother, "Mainly I think she always wants to be your everything. She wants to be your center of attention." While the term *narcissism* was not uniformly used, all of the . . . mothers were portrayed as self-centered, demanding a high degree of attention and admiration, and not able to see their children as separate individuals—the very essence of narcissism. . . . The alienating mothers in these families were portrayed as charming, dynamic, and preoccupied with having their own needs met rather than meeting the needs of their children. These narcissistic mothers cultivated an emotionally enmeshed relationship with the adult children of PAS [parental alienation syndrome] when they were young children,

Research shows that in divorce the mother is often the "custodial alienating parent" who is more concerned with herself than with her children's needs.

which appeared to serve the mothers' need for love and admiration, rather than promoting the emotional health and growth of the children. They were able to instill in their children a sense of awe and admiration. The following comments made by Hannah, Alix, and Veronica, respectively, convey the intensity of their feelings for their mothers, "It was fabulous. I was her daughter. I didn't individuate from her. I did everything for her to make her life better" (Hannah). "I was in my mom's world not my own" (Alix). "We were really good friends. It was brilliant. I used to be called her shadow because we'd do everything together" (Veronica). In a similar vein Walter said, "I'm a mama's boy."

Self-Centered Mothers

Maternal narcissism may have fueled the alienation in at least three ways. First, despite the powerful personality presented to the world, narcissists tend to feel empty inside and easily become enraged at the first sign of humiliation or abandonment. Therefore, it is likely that the end of the marriage triggered in these women feelings of shame and rage that became directed toward the husband. . . . Thus, once the father had left the marriage he became an object of intense devaluation and hatred. This is consistent with the steady stream of negative statements made about the absent father following the divorce. These men were referred to as cheaters, gamblers, rapists, alcoholics, and abusers. Carrie said of her mother, "She would constantly bad-mouth my dad saying that he didn't love us. He wanted to move on with his life with my stepmom and she would make us feel bad for wanting to go there." And Mitch recalled that his mother "said all these terrible things about him my whole life." Amelia's mother, too, denigrated the father, saying, "That he did not want nothing to do with us and that basically he was a very bad person." Thus, the alienation may have been partly motivated by revenge, as if the mothers were saying to their ex-husbands, "If you don't want me you cannot have the children either." . . . Further, the father's interest in having an ongoing relationship with the children (he was not rejecting the children) may also have been experienced as a narcissistic injury. The mothers seemed to wish that if the fathers left them that they should abandon the children as well. Statements such as "Daddy doesn't love us anymore," which conflated the rejection of the mother with the rejection of the children, might be seen as a wish rather than a statement of fact or a criticism of the father. Such comments were common occurrences.

A second underlying motivation of the alienation fueled by the mothers' narcissism may have been anger toward the children for wanting to have a relationship with the father despite the fact that he had rejected the mother. This too might have triggered a feeling of abandonment in these mothers. They seemed to feel that because they were hurt and angry with the father, the children should be as well. . . . If they are displeased with someone, the children should be as well. Julia experienced this: "If she was angry with him then I was supposed to be angry." For this reason, the children's interest in having a relationship with their father following the divorce was experienced as a betrayal and contributed to the mothers' desire to alienate them from their fathers.

Third, the narcissistic mothers might have felt especially alone and fragile following the divorce and might have relied on their children for comfort, companionship, and reassurance. Seen in this light, the time the children spent visiting with the father would have been experienced as a profound loss. To be alone in the house while the children were with the father might have been unbearably lonely and threatening. Many narcissists do not know how to be alone and require an audience to feel real and to reassure them of their value. Serita's mother would ask the children where they'd been and would say, "Oh. I was left on my own and nobody really thinks of me." The children's visitation with their father may have triggered the mother's feelings of loss and anger, which was an underlying motivation to alienate the children from their father.

For all these reasons, the relationship between the children and their fathers following the divorce would have been experienced

"Great news Roger, the court has finally resolved the parental access issue. You can see your father again!" Cartoon by Fran. www.CartoonStock.com.

by the mothers as abandonment, loss, and humiliation. To ward off these threatening and noxious feelings (and perhaps to punish the divorced ex-husband) the mother created a loyalty conflict. Serita felt, "We were made to choose"; and if Maria showed any positive feelings for her father her mother would say, "How could you do this to me? You are betraying me." In having the child choose them over the father, these mothers' emotional needs for revenge, for comfort, for reassurance were satisfied.

Alienating the Other Parent

Thus, the narcissistic mothers convinced their children to reject the targeted parent. . . . Particularly relevant for the discussion of . . . narcissistic mothers are two strategies, described briefly below: cultivation of dependency/threat of rejection and creation of a sense of obligation/guilt. . . .

First, as noted above, the mothers were able to cultivate in their children an unhealthy reliance on their acceptance and approval, much the way cult leaders encourage cult members to become dependent on them. . . . To be out of their mother's favor represented an unimaginable loss for the children. Disapproval was to be avoided at all costs; and this was achieved through compliance with the alienation. Thus, alienation from the father was the price for the mother's approval, a price they were willing to pay in order to avoid her rejection. . . . In these . . . families, in order to obtain the approval of their mother, the children had to relinquish their will, their autonomy, and their relationship with the father.

Typical of narcissists, however, the closeness these mothers cultivated with their children was sustained only as long as they were gratifying the mothers' needs. As soon as the mothers felt wounded or were displeased, the children were devalued and emotionally cut off. Withdrawal of love was particularly conspicuous following visitation with the father. Serita's and Ron's experiences are illustrative, "When I did see him she was horrible to me. When I came back from visits she wouldn't talk to me"; and "My mother would get really angry if, for example, my brother or I displayed any affection for my father." These mothers appeared to alternate between enveloping their children in a loving world in which they basked in the glow of maternal acceptance and exiling their children to a world of coldness and maternal rejection. This vacillation was particularly extreme for Sarah who confided, "I was afraid of her and I was afraid of losing her."

Further, these children observed first hand what happened when someone displeased or challenged their mothers, having witnessed the rage directed toward the father (and, in some cases other people as well, including grandparents, colleagues, and friends). In order to avoid a similar fate, they placed their mother first in their emotional lives. Because they were never sure where they stood and because they believed that they needed their mother's approval for their very survival, they would have done almost anything to please her, including rejecting the father. . . .

Mothers Needing to Be Taken Care Of

Second, the mothers also appeared to their children as fragile and in need of their loyalty and emotional support. They believed that not only were they needed by their mothers but that they somehow owed it to their mothers to take care of them. Sarah's devotion to her mother is illustrative, "I didn't bring any friends home. I felt like I was supposed to be there for my mom all the time. I felt like if I associated with anyone other than her I was betraying her." This dynamic facilitated the alienation because the children believed that rejection of the father was necessary in order to heal the mother or at least stave off further damage and suffering. Thus, these mothers were able to make their feelings and needs more urgent and compelling to their children than not only the father's needs but even their own. Sarah added, "I would see her cry a lot so she appeared very fragile to me so that made me feel more responsible to be there for her." It is possible that such responsibility, although frightening, might also have been gratifying (in part) to these children because it enhanced their sense of power and importance.

ELEVEN

Stepfamilies Present Challenges to Children

Isolina Ricci

Isolina Ricci is a family expert, lecturer, award-winning mediator, and licensed family therapist. She consults in family court and works directly with families. She is the director of the New Family Center in northern California and has authored several books. In her work *Mom's House, Dad's House for Kids*, excerpted below, Ricci argues that adjusting to a new stepfamily does not happen overnight. It is important, she contends, that children give themselves and their stepfamily members time to adjust to their new environment. Children face new challenges with regard to rules and behavior. Ricci argues that there may be different rules for Mom's house, as there will be for Dad's home. Stepparents may have different ideas about how children should be raised. Ricci asserts that until things get worked out, this may be a confusing time for children. To aid in this endeavor, Ricci offers some practical suggestions and guidelines, included in this excerpt, that may help children navigate through the emotional and physical realities of adapting to a new stepfamily.

During the first months or even a year or two, everyone in a stepfamily is learning how to live together and learning about each other. You grew up with your siblings and your parent, but not with your stepfamily members. There is a lot to know. Just like you, they will have favorite foods, movies, music, sports, and hobbies. They will have things that bug them, things that make them smile, and stuff they like to do when they just hang out. They probably also have opinions about the new house rules, routines, and schedules, too—just like you. . . .

WAYS TO GET TO KNOW EACH OTHER BETTER

- Be respectful and courteous.
- Give everyone a chance to be heard and understood.
- Ask questions of one another.
- Offer to help each other out with little things. It's also okay to ask for help.
- Don't put pressure on your stepsiblings or yourself to like each other a lot right away.
- Don't put pressure on your stepparents to treat you like their own kid right away.
- Respect how everyone is different. You're your own person and you are unique. Everyone else in your household is, too.

Remember, even when people like each other a lot, getting along and becoming friends doesn't happen overnight. When people are respectful and courteous, the road to friendship is open. When people are jealous, rude, or snobby, the road to friendship is closed. The same is true in any family, especially in a stepfamily. Eventually you can all feel like a pulled-together family. So, no pressure. Take it easy. Give yourself plenty of time. In the meantime, give everyone in the new family a chance.

Negotiating New Rules

Everyone, no matter in what kind of family, has some kind of house rules. Some families have a lot of rules; others have few. There are usually rules about what people need to do for chores in the house and rules about how to behave. If you had two

Stepfamily Tasks

1. Get to know new family members.
2. Learn how to live together as a new family team.
3. Get used to having a stepparent.
4. Get used to having stepsiblings.
5. Figure out who is boss of what.
6. Figure out which rules and ways of doing things will stay the same and which will change.
7. Figure out consequences if rules and agreements are not followed.
8. Get used to a new room or sharing a room.
9. Get used to a new neighborhood, new home, or school.
10. Welcome a new baby into the family.
11. Have family meetings or discussions to see how things are working out.
12. Learn to trust each other and help that trust to keep growing.

Taken from: Isolina Ricci, "Learning to Live Together" in *Mom's House, Dad's House for Kids: Feeling at Home in One Home or Two*. New York: Simon & Schuster, 2006, pp.143-44.

When adjusting to a new stepfamily, it is important that all members get together to discuss the rules for the new household.

homes, you had one set of rules with Mom and one with Dad. Once you get a stepparent, your rules might change again. Stepparents may have different ideas about what kids should do or not do. If this happens, the adults need to work it out. Until they do, it can be confusing sometimes. So try to be patient.

Rules and Family Meetings

When a family can get together and talk nicely and thoughtfully about rules, it can really help. Daria's mom and stepdad held a family meeting before their wedding and talked about the rules they had in their first families. Then everyone talked about which rules they wanted to keep for their new stepfamily. The parents made the final decisions. The kids didn't all agree with the new rules, but nobody felt left out or picked on. Everyone has to follow the same rules now. The parents decided that each parent could remind any kid of a house rule when that kid needed reminding. Ask your parent if you can all get together and talk over the rules.

Rules About What You Do and Your Attitude

Families, schools, churches, and activities all have rules about behavior, attitude, and how to treat people. It's more than manners.

Rules can be about piercings, nutrition, carrying cash, making up tests at school, clothing choices, team membership, and just about anything else that's about you in the world. Your parents' job is to raise you in a way so your behaviors will support your efforts to be a successful and happy adult. Both your parent and your stepparent may have their own ideas about this. Sometimes your parent, and not your stepparent, will be the only one talking to you about the way you handle yourself.

Different Rules for Different Homes

Some rules are a problem. Here's one. Nadia has really different rules at her mom's and at her dad's. At her dad's, her homework is to be finished with lights-out by 9 P.M. on school nights. But at her mom's, she stays up until 10:30 or sometimes later. Her dad picks her up after soccer, but her mom tells her to take the bus home. At one home she has to be very neat and make her own lunch, at the other home she doesn't. She tries to keep it straight, but she gets mixed up and then she gets in trouble. She doesn't know exactly what she wants, but she wants things to get better. Nadia's stepmom wants Nadia to follow the rules she has for her own kids. Her dad doesn't say anything. Nadia thinks, "She's not my mom and this is unfair. My stepsiblings get to keep their old rules, I don't."

Nadia decided to write her thoughts in a letter. She remembered that people listen and understand better when you start your conversation by saying something good about them. Nadia was feeling mad about the rules. She had to stop and force herself to think of good things to say that were honest. Her bad feelings were crowding out her good memories. . . .

Trouble Among the Parents

Sometimes kids see trouble among all their parents. Ben now hears his stepmom talking to his mom with an angry voice about which school he should attend next year. He's trying to like his stepmom and he loves his mom. He doesn't like it when he hears they have problems, especially about him.

In another family, a dad told his friends in front of his daughter that her new stepdad was a jerk. She felt she had to defend her stepdad, but she didn't know how to do this. She felt disloyal to both of them, but none of this was her fault.

Sometimes adults don't control their strong feelings. They can say and do things that hurt others just like anyone else. If you are in situations like this, you have a choice. You can tell your parents what you heard and how it made you feel, or you can just try to ignore it and say to yourself, "This is an adult problem. I'm not going to try and fix it."

If you do want to say something, think about words something like, "Dad, you know that I love you. But when you called my stepdad a jerk to your friends in front of me, it made me feel really weird." You might ask your parents to stop. Or you might decide it's too risky to say anything and just let it go. You decide what's best. Remember, anytime you try to change how adults talk or treat one another, you are putting yourself in the middle, even when they are arguing about you. . . .

Every family has disagreements. It doesn't matter if the parents are single, divorced, or remarried. For example, a parent or stepparent might want to add new chores to the schedule. But the kids might expect that things will be the same as they were before the stepfamily began. Everyone can have ideas about what others should or should not do. At first these different ideas can bump into one another. It can be a pot of feeling soup.

TWELVE

Family Therapy Can Benefit Children

Anne C. Bernstein

Anne C. Bernstein is a professor at the Wright Institute. She is in private practice as a family psychologist and mediator. Her clinical and research interests include stepfamilies, divorce and remarriage, adoption, collaborative reproduction, and cultural diversity. She is the associate editor for the Web site of *Family Process*. She has authored many books, including *Yours, Mine, and Ours: How Families Change When Remarried Parents Have a Child Together.* In "Re-visioning, Restructuring, and Reconciliation: Clinical Practice with Complex Postdivorce Families," excerpted below, Bernstein argues that although reconciliation may not be possible for some families, postdivorce therapy can be an important first step in healing the wounds imposed on the parent-child relationship during divorce. It is important, she states, that in trying to repair these damaged relationships, parents listen to the anguish and pain they have inflicted on their children, without judgment and self-justification. At the same time, children must confront their loss and pain and let go of their feelings of anger and resentment before they can reconcile with their parents. Bernstein argues that just because marital separation confers emotional wounds, it does not necessarily imply that those wounds cannot be healed. In one case, included in this excerpt, Bernstein gives an account of her attempts to reconcile twenty-two-year-old Jeanne with her forty-five-year-old father, Jim, with whom she is staying while waiting to enter medical school.

As someone who has worked extensively with estranged parent-child dyads and divorced parents, I find the concepts of self-injurious spite and accusatory suffering all too familiar. Teenagers and young adults especially may embrace the Child of Divorce narrative as a damaged identity. Thus, they may dismiss out of hand parental efforts to alleviate their distress, isolate themselves in the stepfamily, develop symptoms that are a constant reminder that the parent has inflicted harm, or decline all invitations to improve living conditions. And, even when they feel little or no control of symptoms or choice about isolation, they may not be ready to relinquish such symptoms as vexing obsessive rituals and are surprisingly open to admitting that they do not want the minor improvements parents can provide. When asked, "I wonder if you don't want to let her make it better because then she won't 'get' how miserable she's made you by [leaving a marriage, moving in with a new partner, and so on]?" they often agree. . . .

Wounds That Do Not Heal

Estrangement stemming from a sense of injury—be it major or minor, intentional or inadvertent, physical or symbolic—does not heal rapidly or, in most instances, without considerable effort. Some ruptured relationships are never repaired, but family therapy can bridge—not close—the gap in a surprising number of postdivorce families. The work calls on all the resources that family therapy brings to the table: the ability to think systemically, listen with sensitivity and respect for the experience of all

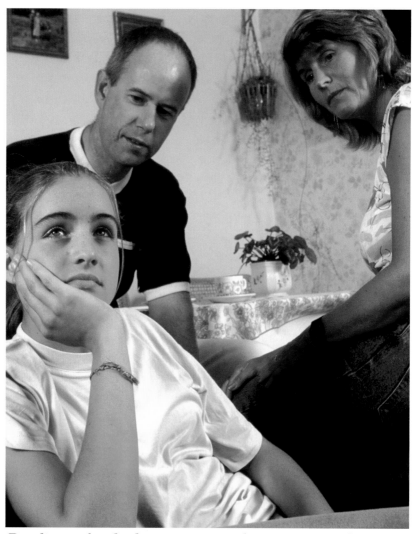

Postdivorce family therapy stresses the importance of sensitivity to and respect for other family members in order to reach the goal of forgiveness and reconciliation.

family members, to create a safe place to raise heuristic questions that engage participants' curiosity, and to educate—both convey information and draw out the potential for beneficence. Emphasizing the distinction between forgiveness and reconciliation, as one example, can assist ex-spouses in taking the initial steps to cooperatively coparent.

In working with damaged parent-child relationships, the parent listening nondefensively to the child's pain as the child acknowledges the loss is an important part of repairing relations. . . .

Accepting that marital transitions, however well handled, are also emotionally bruising doesn't mean that the bruises cannot heal when they are aired and treated tenderly. Supporting the telling and witnessing of "truths" is an important part of the therapeutic process of facilitating reconciliation, the "restoration of wholeness or harmony."

Case Example: The Tyler Family

The Tylers are a stepfamily created by the remarriage of two teachers. In the year between college and medical school, Jeanne, 22, was living full time with her father, Jim, 45, for the first time since her parents separated a dozen years earlier. Father and daughter sought therapy to repair their relationship, strained by a conflictual divorce and the difficulties that both experienced in making Jeanne a part of the family that he had formed with his new wife, her son, now 15, and their twin daughters, 9. Tearfully, Jeanne reported that her needs had long been ignored or subordinated to those of the full-time residents. As a child, she had felt "lonely in a crowd" at Dad's, often calling her mother to retrieve her early, leaving over Dad's objections to return to the quieter home she shared with Mom. Now, both feel that the old story of childhood hurt and paternal frustration is being replayed.

Much of the therapy consisted of working on the pattern of mutual defensiveness. Jeanne wanted to feel that her father loves her and that she is important to him. Instead, she felt unwelcome and peripheral, finding his actions unresponsive and his words invalidating. Jim wanted his daughter to feel comfortably a part of his family and to find him a "good enough" father, imperfect certainly, but loving and not out to hurt her. Instead, he felt that his efforts were dismissed as inadequate. Each anticipated the other's response and attributed to it ill will or lack of charity. Each felt negatively caricatured by the other and, as a result, both were less friendly than each would like to have been. Their reciprical negative inferences became untested but tenacious beliefs.

By slowing down the dialogue, I worked to make the attributions transparent. Because each heard the other's experience as an accusation, each acknowledged the other only briefly ("I know you were hurt") before going on to counter the implied or overt accusation ("but I . . .") at greater length. What lingered was the self-justification; the acknowledgement passed so quickly that it failed to register. I interrupted their dialogue to ask each to both amplify their acknowledgement of the other and ascertain that it was received. The pattern of interlocking sensitivities was such that when a "button was pushed," the entire message in which it was embedded was discounted. At one point, Jim made a heartfelt declaration of his continuing love and commitment, lamenting that he had not successfully communicated his caring to Jeanne. She responded that he was saying that she should not feel as she does. I asked her to entertain the possibility that both could be true—that he cares and that

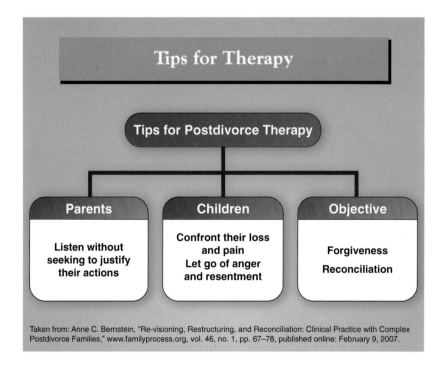

Taken from: Anne C. Bernstein, "Re-visioning, Restructuring, and Reconciliation: Clinical Practice with Complex Postdivorce Families," www.familyprocess.org, vol. 46, no. 1, pp. 67–78, published online: February 9, 2007.

she does not experience him as caring—and invited their curiosity as to how that may have come about. Jim then described how he had learned a typically masculine pattern from his own father: responding to hurt by adopting a "you're not getting to me" attitude.

Making direct statements about one's responses and needs is the reciprocal of being curious about those of the other. Long having seen Jeanne as "too sensitive," Jim needed to differentiate reasonable requests that deserved accommodation from what he perceived as a web of implied indictments. He resolved to change his characteristic response when he could not be immediately available to her, agreeing to cite a future time that he would be free to meet rather than simply cataloguing what he had to do with whom—a response that always left Jeanne feeling that she came last in the family.

Jim asked Jeanne to be direct in asking for attention rather than looking for openings and angrily withdrawing when she saw none. She insisted that just because she has the potential to be more direct now does not mean that it was in her power to get what she needed earlier. Differentiating between what was possible for her in adulthood from what had been developmentally inaccessible to her as a child opened the way to create reparative experiences. Without this distinction, however, it was clear that she would not have been able to betray her childhood reality by trying something different.

Not all families can move beyond the old hurts, disappointments, sense of betrayal, and the injuries—psychosocial, economic, or physical—that often accompany divorce. For some, what approximates reconciliation only comes years down the road, occasioned by the illness or death of a family member, the wedding of a child, or the birth of a grandchild. For others, "parallel parenting"—taking care of one's children with minimal contact between exes or resorting to a third party for communication—is all that can be achieved. Yet for a surprising number of postdivorce families, including those who least expect it, mutually respectful relationships are attainable with time, inclination, and effort.

THIRTEEN

Children of Divorce Are More Likely to Divorce

Nicholas H. Wolfinger

Nicholas H. Wolfinger is an associate professor in the Department of Family and Consumer Studies at the University of Utah and an adjunct associate professor in the Department of Sociology at the University of Utah. He is the coeditor of the book *Fragile Families and the Marriage Agenda* and has published widely in journals such as *Demography*, *Social Forces*, and the *Journal of Family Issues*. In his recent work, *Understanding the Cycle of Divorce*, Wolfinger argues that more than any other reason, lack of commitment contributes to the cycle of divorce within families. He asserts that besides teaching children that marital conflicts are resolved by dissolving marriage, parental divorce gives legitimacy to the notion that marriage is not permanent and that one can simply opt out of the marital union when troubles arise. Children of divorce in particular, he adds, might choose to end their marriages simply because they are emotionally incapable of dealing with marital conflicts that are innate to most marriages. Consequently, they will ultimately dissolve their own marriages. In addition, Wolfinger claims that the correlation between the parents' divorce and their

Nicholas H. Wolfinger, *Understanding the Divorce Cycle: The Children of Divorce in Their Own Marriages*. New York: Cambridge University Press, 2005. Copyright © Cambridge University Press 2005. Reprinted with the permission of Cambridge University Press.

offsprings' divorces can often be traced to behaviors displayed by the children themselves. Citing research outlined in this excerpt, Wolfinger argues that children of divorce cannot maintain a marital relationship because they manifest behaviors that are hostile and adverse to marriage, such as uncontrolled anger, the desire to dominate, and the tendency to be critical and judgmental. This suggests, Wolfinger argues, that for children of parental divorce, marriage constitutes an entirely different experience than it does for children from intact marriages.

M ost people will be able to provide a ready answer if asked why divorce has negative effects on children: "Kids need fathers" is one likely response. But the absence or presence of a male role model is not what matters most, it seems. Divorce often subjects children to potentially harmful conflict. Moreover, one- and two-parent families have very different economic circumstances, live in different kinds of neighborhoods, and provide children with different home environments. Which of these factors is responsible for the divorce cycle? . . .

Role Modeling Redux

Instead of learning about marital commitment from their parents, the children of divorce may instead learn about marital dissolution. There are several variations on this theme. One of them, the notion that parental divorce reduces offspring marital commitment, turns out to be the most likely explanation for the divorce cycle that has been offered to date. . . .

Parental divorce reduces offspring commitment to marriage, rather than simply legitimating dissolution as a solution for marital difficulties. As a result, the children of divorce become likely to opt out of troubled marriages. Subtly different from the notion of legitimation, low commitment to marriage is the most convincing argument for the divorce cycle proposed to date.

Children who have experienced their parents' divorce may have difficulty handling marriage themselves and are more likely to divorce than people from stable families.

Almost every marriage has rough spots, but most couples manage to weather the storm. Numerous forces conspire to prevent divorce, including children, social expectations, the legal and religious ramifications of matrimony, financial considerations, and commitment built over time. Perhaps a history of parental divorce changes all that. If relationships seem unstable, they also may seem unsalvageable. The children of divorce may be especially likely to end their own marriages simply because they are ill-equipped to endure the hardships inherent in romantic relationships. Reduced commitment therefore reflects a malfunction that undermines marriage, as opposed to the willful acceptance of divorce as a useful strategy for resolving a troubled relationship. This distinguishes explanations for the divorce cycle based on the intergenerational transmission of reduced commitment from arguments founded on an increased acceptance of marital dissolution. . . .

Divorce Begets Divorce

Paul Amato and Danelle DeBoer . . . show that people are most likely to divorce when their parents' divorces were preceded by low levels of marital conflict. Children under these circumstances presumably learn lessons about both dealing with interpersonal difficulties and the relative impermanence of marriage: If a marriage runs into trouble, the best solution is to call it quits right away. No other means of resolving the problem may seem tenable. In contrast, offspring experiencing divorce after enduring high levels of parental conflict learn to persist with their own relationships even when difficulties arise.

One manifestation of low commitment might be an exaggerated perception of marital difficulties. The children of divorce often feel that their marriages are in trouble, even though on average their unions are no less happy than the marriages of people who grew up in intact families. A feeling of impending marital doom very well may be the harbinger of a "low commitment" divorce. . . .

Another useful piece of evidence in accounting for the relationship between marital commitment and the divorce cycle is the effect of stepparenting. People whose divorced parents remarry are especially likely to end their own marriages. This finding is consistent with the more general literature on stepparenting, which shows that remarriage does not ameliorate the negative consequences of parental divorce. Although it has not been confirmed that parental remarriage reduces offspring marital commitment, the connection is easily made. By his or

her very presence, a stepparent shows that divorce does not signify an irremediable loss; another spouse can always be obtained.
In short, the lesson children learn about marriage is easy come,
easy go.

Parental Divorce and Offspring Marital Problems

Based on the evidence considered thus far, low marital commitment stands out as the most likely explanation for the divorce
cycle. Although this answers the question of why divorce transmission occurs, it falls short of explaining how. Here we must
turn to a separate body of literature. Considerable evidence now
shows that impaired interpersonal skills play a key role in explaining why people from divorced families have so much trouble in their own marriages. Once marriages strained by
problematic interpersonal skills enter a crisis period, low commitment to marriage prevents these couples from resolving their
differences.

Table 2.1. *Some Marital Behaviors Observed in the
Children of Divorce*

From Amato (1996: 633–4):
  1) Gets angry easily
  2) Has feelings that are easily hurt
  3) Is jealous
  4) Is domineering
  5) Is critical
  6) Won't talk to the other (spouse)
  7) Has had a sexual relationship with someone else
  8) Has irritating habits
  9) Is not home enough
10) Spends money foolishly

From Webster, Orbuch, and House (1995; Table 4):
  1) Shouts when arguing
  2) Keeps opinions to self
  3) Does not calmly discuss disagreements

From Silvestri (1992: 104):
1) Maladjustment in modesty (too self-critical)
2) Submissiveness (docile, dependent, passive behaviors)
3) Distrustfulness
4) Maladjustment in responsibility (too much or not enough)
5) Inability to self-evaluate
6) Uncooperativeness
7) Hostile passive behavior

Source: Wolfinger (2000), 1064.

Paul Amato has conducted the most significant piece of research in this area. He found that the relationship between parental divorce and offspring divorce could largely be explained by a problem behavior scale composed of ten items. These ten items are shown in the first panel of Table 2.1. A study by Webster, Orbuch, and House also identified marital traits common to people from divorced families though they did not ascertain how these traits contribute to the risk of divorce. These traits appear in the second panel of Table 2.1. A third list of problematic marital behaviors comes from research by Silvio Silvestri. All three lists reflect significant differences between adult children from intact families and adult children of divorce.

The contents of the three lists vary because each study analyzed a different data set. There are some contradictions: "Domineering" appears on Amato's list, while "submissive" is on Silvestri's. Some of the characteristics listed, especially "has irritating habits," are sufficiently vague as to have little useful meaning. For these reasons, it would be difficult to develop a clinical profile of marital behavior in the children of divorce based on these three lists. Taken together, they make a single basic point: The children of divorce often display behaviors that are inimical to maintaining a relationship. Further evidence for this point comes from three studies that have linked parental marital conflict with offspring marital conflict. By almost any definition, conflict is problematic marital behavior.

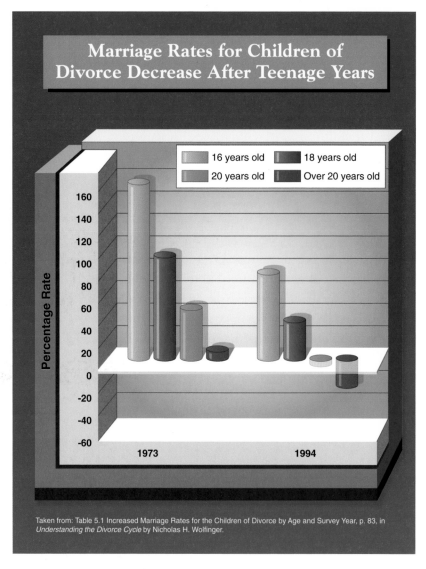

Marriage Rates for Children of Divorce Decrease After Teenage Years

Legend: 16 years old, 18 years old, 20 years old, Over 20 years old

Percentage Rate axis: 160, 140, 120, 100, 80, 60, 40, 20, 0, -20, -40, -60

1973   1994

Taken from: Table 5.1 Increased Marriage Rates for the Children of Divorce by Age and Survey Year, p. 83, in *Understanding the Divorce Cycle* by Nicholas H. Wolfinger.

At first glance, these findings appear to contradict the fact that the children of divorce do not report lower levels of happiness in their own marriages than do people from intact families. How can marriages strained by conflict or interpersonal difficulties be happy? The answer is that the children of divorce must have a different understanding of marital happiness than do people from intact families: At the very least, offspring from divorced families view marriage less favorably than do people who did not experience parental divorce. Moreover, as noted earlier the children of divorce often feel their marriages are in trouble even when they are happy. All of this suggests that marriage is a much different experience for the children of divorce than it is for people from intact families. . . .

This understanding sheds light on the relationship between interpersonal difficulties and low marital commitment. Recall that growing up in an acrimonious but intact family increases the likelihood of difficulties in one's own marriage but has little effect on divorce rates. Similarly, parental divorce increases the incidence of problematic behaviors within the marriages of adult offspring, but this in itself may not be sufficient to trigger the divorce cycle. Problematic interpersonal behaviors can certainly strain a relationship, but with sufficient resolve couples may opt to stay married. Add low commitment to the marriage and dissolution becomes much more likely. Parental divorce provides the key ingredient necessary to lower the commitment of offspring, thereby transforming a troubled marriage into a divorce-prone marriage.

What You Should Know About Divorce and Children

Facts About Divorce

According to the U.S. Census Bureau:

- Approximately 2,230,000 people were married in 2005—down from 2,279,000 the previous year, despite a total population increase of 2.9 million over the same period.
- The divorce rate in 2005 (per 1,000 people) was 3.6—the lowest rate since 1970, and down from 4.2 in 2000 and from 4.7 in 1990. (The peak was at 5.3 in 1981, according to the Associated Press.)
- In 2004 the state with the highest reported divorce rate was Nevada, at 6.4 (per 1,000). Arkansas was a close second, with a divorce rate of 6.3, followed by Wyoming at 5.3. The District of Columbia had the lowest reported divorce rate, at 1.7, followed by Massachusetts at 2.2 and Pennsylvania at 2.5. (Figures were not complete for California, Georgia, Hawaii, Indiana, Louisiana, or Oklahoma.)
- 8.1 percent of coupled households consist of unmarried heterosexual partners, according to *The State of Our Unions 2005*, a report issued by the National Marriage Project at Rutgers University. The same study said that only 63 percent of American children grow up with both biological parents—the lowest figure in the Western world.
- As of 2003, 43.7 percent of custodial mothers and 56.2 percent of custodial fathers were either separated or divorced. And in 2002, 7.8 million Americans paid about $40 billion

in child and/or spousal support (84 percent of the payers were male).

- Americans tend to get married more between June and October than during the rest of the year. In 2005 August had the most marriages at about 235,000 or a rate of 9.3 per 1,000 people. The previous year July was the highest month at 246,000, or a rate of 9.9; this doubled the lowest month in 2004, January.

How Divorce Impacts Children:

According to studies done by prominent social scientists, parental divorce impacts children in different ways and in different stages of their lives. For children between the ages of 13 and18, parental divorce may have the following consequences:

- Difficulty managing and expressing feelings of anger, outrage, shame, and sadness
- Difficulty in adjusting to parental divorce, which may result in running away, truancy, and delinquency
- Poor interpersonal relationships with peers and the opposite sex
- Poor school performance
- Early sexual activity
- Higher rate of alcohol and drug abuse

Long-Term Impact of Divorce on Children

According to Judith S. Wallerstein, parental divorce has far-reaching consequences for children that go well beyond their adolescent years and into adulthood. As a result, in their late twenties and early forties children of divorce struggle to overcome the following:

- Fear of commitment
- Fear of betrayal
- Expectation that their own marriage will end in divorce
- Inability to handle conflict in their own relationships since this may lead to the impulse to escape
- Fear of being alone leads to self-destructive choices in partners
- Fear of change

What You Should Do About Divorce

According to recent studies, over 1 million children in the United States will experience the divorce of their parents this year. These children typically experience, or have experienced, a whole range of emotions, from heart-wrenching sadness to confusion, anger, and fear. They may feel abandoned and alone or even guilty about the breakup of their parents' marriage. According to social scientists, divorce affects all children differently and to varying degrees of intensity. But the fact is, no matter what the emotional response, divorce is a personal tragedy for all children. Children may feel that their life is completely out of control. Yet despite the instability and challenges that children face, they can do many things to lead happier and fuller lives following the divorce of their parents.

To begin with, teenagers must realize they cannot force their parents to reunite, no matter how much they may long for this to happen. Richard M. Kingsley in "A Kid's Guide to Divorce" states that some children feel that if they try hard enough at home and at school, somehow this will bring their parents back together. He adds that although many parents would be immensely proud of their child's achievements, this will not change their decision to end their marriage. Conversely, children may purposely act out or get into trouble so that their parents will be forced to interact with each other, and in doing so, see the futility of their decision to divorce. Unfortunately, Kingsley contends, this too will do little to change their parents' minds.

Another important tactic for children of divorce is to communicate about the divorce to either a parent or a friend. This is an important part of the recovery process. Reaching out helps alleviate some of the pain. If talking seems difficult, writing in a journal can also be therapeutic. Michelle New in "A Teen's Guide to Divorce" argues that if these feelings of sadness or depression persist or interfere with a child's ability to function, he or she may need to talk to a professional counselor. Turning to their parents or school counselors for help in finding a good therapist, or even a support group, is a good idea, she adds.

Children should find the time to talk to both parents on a regular basis, especially to the noncustodial parent. Therapists contend that keeping in constant communication with loved ones lessens some of the sadness and pain.

Children need to avoid getting in the middle of parental conflicts. Psychologists know that sometimes when parents split up, they force children to take sides or make them feel guilty if they want a relationship with the other parent as well. For most children, this is intolerable. Moreover, adolescents are not and should not be made to feel responsible for their parent's happiness.

Do not tolerate parental squabbling. Children find it unsettling to cope with their parents' bickering and arguing. Many psychologists argue, however, that children have more power than they think. Children may be powerless to stop their parents from seeking a divorce, but they are not powerless to act in their own best interest. Children should be vocal and ask their parents to refrain from bickering and fighting in front of them and to treat each other with courtesy and respect.

Children should not hesitate to talk to parents about their fears for the future. For many children, who may themselves be experiencing physiological and emotional changes, the divorce of their parents can be completely devastating. With their families torn asunder, teenagers face the future with great uncertainty. Who will provide for me? Will my parents really be there for me, emotionally or financially? Will I have the things I need to complete high school? Will my parents support me through college? Many therapists contend that for their own emotional health and well-being, it is important that children discuss their anxiety about the future with their parents, regardless of how their parents may feel or react.

Children also need to stay active and involved. It is a common belief that in times of great stress, keeping daily activities as normal as possible will prevent things from spinning out of control. And this is true of divorce. Although life may be chaotic and unstable when parents divorce, it is imperative that children stay active and involved in school and in whatever sports and community activities they normally participate in and attend. In addition, children need to take special care of themselves during this stressful time by exercising daily and eating a healthy diet.

Finally, children need to realize that they are resilient. Conflicts provide opportunities for growth. And so it is with the challenges of divorce. Some psychologists argue that learning to cope with irate parents who are constantly yelling at each other, for example, may provide the opportunity for teenagers to control their own emotions and to later address their parents' behavior in a quiet, rational manner. In refusing to get caught up in the emotional roller coaster that often occurs in an unstable environment, teenagers will soon realize that they do indeed have strengths, and that with these coping skills, they will survive this unhappy period in their lives.

Divorce is a destabilizing time for all children, especially for teenagers. But there is hope. By reaching out to others they trust, letting their parents know how they feel, focusing their lives, and believing in themselves, teenagers can lead happier and fuller lives.

ORGANIZATIONS TO CONTACT

The editors have compiled the following list of organizations concerned with the issues debated in this book. The descriptions are derived from materials provided by the organizations. All have publications or information available for interested readers. The list was compiled on the date of publication of the present volume; the information provided here may change. Be aware that many organizations take several weeks or longer to respond to inquiries, so allow as much time as possible.

American Coalition for Fathers and Children (ACFC)
1718 M St. NW, Ste.187, Washington, DC 20036
(800) 978-3237
Web site: www.acfc.org

ACFC's aim is to restore equal rights to fathers affected by divorce, family breakup, and childbirth out of wedlock.

Association for Children for Enforcement of Support (ACES)
2260 Upton Ave., Toledo, OH 43606
(800) 537-7072
e-mail: aces@childsupport-aces.org
Web site: www.childsupport-aces.org

This is a self-help, nonprofit child-support organization. The association teaches custodial parents what they need to do to collect child support. It has 350 chapters all across the United States. Call, write, or e-mail for information on how to contact a chapter in your area.

The Beginning Experience
International Ministry Center
1657 Commerce Dr., South Bend, IN 46628
(866) 610-8877
Web site: www.beginningexperience.org

The Beginning Experience offers support programs for divorced, widowed, and separated adults and their children, enabling them to work through the grief of a lost marriage.

Children's Rights Council (CRC)
220 I St. NE, Ste. 200, Washington, DC 20002
(202) 547-6227
Web site: www.crckids.org

A national, nonprofit organization, CRC is dedicated to assisting children of separation and divorce through advocacy and parenting education.

Joint Custody Association
10606 Wilkins Ave., Los Angeles, CA 90024
(310) 475-5352
Web site: www.jointcustody.org

The association helps divorcing parents and their families achieve joint custody. It disseminates information concerning family law research and judicial decisions. The association also lobbies for improvement of family law in state legislatures.

National Family Resiliency Center
2000 Century Plaza, Ste. 121, Columbia, MD 21044
(410) 740-9553
Web site: www.divorceABC.com

The National Family Resiliency Center provides parents and professionals with programs and resources to help them navigate the emotionally challenging process of separation, divorce, and remarriage. The center helps children better understand and accept the realities of life-changing experiences in their family, as well as provides the guidance they need in order to identify and express their feelings in a healthy way.

Stepfamily Foundation
333 West End Ave., New York, NY 10023
(800) 759-7837
Web site: www.stepfamily.org

The Stepfamily Foundation is an organization devoted to helping stepfamilies function successfully. The Web site offers information to support those living in complex family systems.

BIBLIOGRAPHY

Books and Periodicals

Jen Abbas, *Generation X: Adult Children of Divorce and the Healing of Our Pain*. Colorado Springs, CO: Waterbook, 2004.

Constance Ahrons, *The Good Divorce—Keeping Your Family Together When Your Marriage Comes Apart*. New York: HarperCollins, 1994.

————, *We're Still Family: What Grown Children Have to Say About Their Parents' Divorce*. New York: HarperCollins, 2004.

Paul R. Amato, "Children of Divorce in the 1900s: An Update of the Amato and Keith (1991) Meta-Analysis," *Journal of Family Psychology*, vol. 15, no. 3, September 2001.

————, "The Consequences of Divorce for Adults and Children," *Journal of Marriage and Family*, vol. 26, no. 4, November 2000.

Paul R. Amato and Alan Booth, *A Generation at Risk: Growing Up in an Era of Family Upheaval*. Cambridge, MA: Harvard University Press, 1997.

Paul R. Amato and Jacob Cheadle, "The Long Reach of Divorce: Divorce and Child Well-Being Across Three Generations," *Journal of Marriage and Family*, vol. 67, no.1, February 2005.

Alan Booth and Paul R. Amato, "Parental Predivorce Relations and Offspring Postdivorce Well-Being," *Journal of Marriage and Family*, vol. 63, no. 1, February 2001.

Alan Booth et al., "Postdivorce Father-Adolescent Closeness," *Journal of Marriage and Family*, vol. 69, no. 5, December 2007.

Christy M. Buchanan, Eleanor M. Maccoby, and Sanford M. Dombusch, *Adolescents After Divorce*. Cambridge, MA: Harvard University Press, 1996.

Lynn Cassella, *Making Your Way After Your Parents' Divorce: A Supportive Guide for Personal Growth*. Ligouri, MO: Ligouri Lifespan, 2002.

Ava Chin, *Divorce*. New York: McGraw Hill, 2002.

Ava Chin, ed., *Stories from a Generation Raised on Divorce*. New York: McGraw Hill, 2002.

Robert Emery, *Renegotiating Family Relationships: Divorce, Child Custody, and Mediation*. New York: Guilford, 1994.

Paula Fomby and Andrew J. Cherlin, "Family Instability and Child Well-Being," *American Sociological Review*, April 2007.

Frank F. Furstenberg Jr. and Andrew J. Cherlin, *Divided Families: What Happens to Children When Parents Part*. Cambridge, MA: Harvard University Press, 1991.

Joseph Helmrich and Paul Marcus, *Warring Parents, Wounded Children, and the Wretched World of Child Custody*. Westport, CT: Greenwood, 2007.

Martin Herbert, *Separation and Divorce: Helping Children Cope*. Malden, MA: Blackwell, 1996.

Sara R. Jaffee et al., "Life with (or Without) Father: The Benefits of Living with Two Biological Parents Depends on the Father's Antisocial Behavior," *Child Development*, vol. 74, July 2003.

Janet R. Johnston et al., *Through the Eyes of Children*. New York: Simon & Schuster, 1997.

Katherine Krohn, *You and Your Parents' Divorce*. New York: Rosen, 2001.

Jennifer E. Lansford et al., "Trajectories of Internalizing, Externalizing, and Grades for Children Who Have and Have Not Experienced Their Parents' Divorce and Separation," *Journal of Family Psychology*, vol. 20, no. 2, June 2006.

Liana Lowenstein, *Creative Inventions for Children of Divorce*. Toronto: Champion, 2006.

Elizabeth Marquardt, *Between Two Worlds: The Inner Lives of Children of Divorce*. New York: Crown, 2006.

Jennifer McIntosh, "Enduring Conflict in Parental Separation: Pathways of Impact on Child Development," *Journal of Family Studies*, vol. 9, no. 1, April 2003.

Sara McLanahan and Gary Sandefur, *Growing Up with a Single Parent: What Hurts, What Helps*. Cambridge, MA: Harvard University Press, 1994.

Jane D. McLeod and Karen Kaiser, "Childhood Emotional and Behavioural Problems in Educational Attainment," *American Sociological Review*, October 2004.

David Popenoe, *Life Without Father: Compelling New Evidence That Fatherhood and Marriage Are Indispensable for the Good of Children and Society*. New York: Free Press, 1996.

S.M. Portnoy, "The Psychology of Divorce: A Lawyer's Primer, Part 2: The Effects of Divorce on Children," *American Journal of Family Law*, vol. 21, no. 4, 2008.

Meg F. Schneider and Joan Zuckerberg, *Difficult Questions Kids Ask and Are Afraid to Ask About Divorce*. New York: Simon & Schuster, 1996.

Stephanie Staal, *The Love They Lost: Living with the Legacy of Our Parents' Divorce*. New York: Delacorte, 2000.

Judith S. Wallerstein and Sandra Blakeslee, *What About the Kids? Raising Your Children Before, During, and After Divorce*. New York: Hyperion, 2003.

Web Sites

Dealing with Divorce, TeensHealth (http://kidshealth.org/teen/your_mind/families/divorce.html). Provides accurate and up-to-date information on divorce and health and what children can do to overcome this sad and unstable period in their lives.

Divorce Kids: A Child's Perspective (www.divorce-kids.com). Helps children realize that they are not alone when it comes to custody; many other children are facing the same challenges.

It's Not Your Fault (www.itsnotyourfault.org). Offers help for young people whose parents are splitting up.

Surviving Your Parents' Divorce (www.survivingyourparentsdivorce.com). Debuting his new Web site, the author of *The Bright Side:*

Surviving Your Parents Divorce helps children with advice and insight on how to turn their parents' divorce into a positive experience for themselves.

Teen Center: Divorce, Whole Family.com (www.wholefamily. com/aboutteensnow/relationships_family/index.html#divorce). Provides teenagers with resources and advice from a team of experts and professionals that enables them to face the challenges of their parents' divorce and make good decisions.

PICTURE CREDITS